DIARY OF A FUTURE BILLIONAIRE

PAMELA BUTCHART

DIARY OF A FUTURE BILLIONAIRE

ILLUSTRATED BY

WOTTO

SCHOLASTIC

Published in the UK by Scholastic, 2025
Scholastic, Bosworth Avenue, Warwick, CV34 6UQ

ISBN 978-93-5954-925-5

A CIP catalogue record for this book is available from the British Library.

This reprint edition: June, 2025

www.scholastic.co.uk

For safety or quality concerns:
UK: www.scholastic.co.uk/productinformation
EU: www.scholastic.ie/productinformation

Printed in India at Nutech Print Services - India

FOR ALBIE

So here's the thing about me. I'm Ben and I'm a **BILLIONAIRE**. An actual **REAL-LIFE** billionaire!

And you know how some people who get rich say stuff like "I can't believe it!" and "I never thought it would happen to me!"?

Well ... I can believe it.

And I knew it would happen to me.

Because I planned it.

I planned to become the world's richest ten-year-old.

And you know what?

It **WORKED**.

OK, well, I'm not actually a billionaire yet.

But I **AM** getting richer.

Here's my diary to record how it's going.

Want to come along for the ride?

Read on if the answer is **YES** (and if you're curious about what a mongoose is...).

A NOTE FROM THE AUTHOR

I'm not surprised that a big publishing company wants to publish my **DIARY**.

I guess loads of kids want to become rich. But do they ever actually make it happen?

People often ask me how it all started. And I bet you want to know too...

Well, I'll tell you. It started when Mum made a **DISGUSTING** vegetable stew.

It was horrendous. When Mum put it down in front of me at our kitchen table, I just looked at the bowl and didn't say anything.

I mean, the dinner ladies at school wouldn't even be allowed to serve it, and they serve us soggy broccoli burgers.

"What's wrong, Ben?" Mum asked.

Mum's eyes had gone **WEIRD**, like they do before she starts crying.

And that's when I asked for ketchup.

I waited.

Mum doesn't like it when you ask for salt or ketchup before you've even tried her food.

She says it's **INSULTING** to the chef.

But I had to try something because I was pretty sure that the fumes coming from the stew were starting to blind me.

Mum blinked, then blinked again. My mum doesn't moan or shout... She **CRIES** (which is way worse).

I once made the mistake of telling her I didn't want her to hold my hand when we were crossing the road near school when I was nine, and she cried so hard that the lollipop lady actually put down her lollipop stick and gave Mum a hug.

To this day the lollipop lady gives me a side-eye look every time I see her and I'm pretty sure she thinks I'm the worst son in the world.

I tried to think of something else to say before the tears began pouring down Mum's face. But then she smiled and got the ketchup bottle from the fridge.

It had worked for once. My ketchup needs were met and – double win – Mum didn't cry.

I looked down at the **TERRIBLE** stew and reality kicked in.

I still had to eat it.

Mum had started making **£1 MEALS** when Dad lost all our money. More about that in a moment.

"Can I take my stew through to the living room and sit with Dad?" I said.

Mum looked at me like I'd just slapped her in the face. It was a whole lot worse than offending her by asking for ketchup.

"You don't want to eat with me?" she said, her lip starting to wobble.

The truth is that I did want to eat with her because she was listening to her daily dose of true-crime podcast. Even though she would never let me watch something about murder on TV, she didn't seem to mind me listening to it in the kitchen.

Mum's a writer so she likes to listen for research. She doesn't get paid for it yet, but she REALLY wants to have a book published one day. It's her dream. Mum used to work in Tesco before she had **BABY ANGEL** (yes, that's my sister's real name), but now she looks after my little sister and works on her book.

Mum says writing relaxes her and that she just takes a deep breath and writes whatever comes naturally.

She won't let me read any of it, but Aunty Gemma says it's really good.

Dad says it's a bit too dark for him.

Anyway I didn't actually want to sit in the living room with Dad, because none of us were speaking to him right now. Not Mum, not me and not my baby sister Angel (and not just because she can't speak much). But I DID want to put a lot of ketchup on the disgusting stew.

I told Mum that I wanted to eat with her but that Dad was watching a programme I wanted to see (**WINK, WINK**) and also that I needed to sit on the sofa because my back was hurting (and that last part was actually true because April May had launched herself at me full force during a pretty violent game of rounders in PE that afternoon).

April May is one of those girls who's really good at everything, but she doesn't act like she's better than everyone else (like some of the girls in my class do).

She doesn't try to fit in like all the other girls. She just sort of does her own thing (which actually makes her more popular!).

But April May **DOES** care **A LOT** about winning rounders, though!

Mum thought for a second and then said, "Fine."

I waited a moment without moving, in case she was going to follow up her "fine" with a side of tears.

But she just turned up her podcast and the words **"FOUR SEVERED FINGERS"** blasted out.

So that felt like a good time to leave.

Dad's eyes went really wide when I walked into the living room with my stew.

He didn't say anything, but patted the sofa with a big grin on his face like he'd won the lottery or something.

I had no idea what programme he was watching.

I sat down and opened the bottle of ketchup and started to **COVER** the stew.

Then I did a **SECOND** layer.

Dad looked at the bottle, then at me.

Normally, Dad would definitely have something to say about me using all the ketchup like that! Too much sugar, yadda yadda.

But I guess that when you spend all your family's **SAVINGS** on a **MONGOOSE FARM** and your family can't go on holiday ever again (not even to that caravan that smelled like sick), then you can't really moan about your son using all the ketchup, can you?

I remembered what I'd overheard Mum say on the phone to Aunty Gemma a few weeks ago:

"He's spent it all! **ALL OF IT!** We've been saving that money for years. It was for rent and emergencies! And now it's gone ... and we own a **MONGOOSE FARM!**"

None of us even knew what a mongoose was.

Dad said **HE** knew what a mongoose was, but when Mum handed him a pen and told him to "draw a mongoose" he couldn't do it.

I asked my friend Bilal to try, and he drew this weird face, which looked a bit like a person with loads of eyelashes and a big, surprised O for a mouth.

Apparently he's trying this new art style called **ABSTRACT**. We did a class on abstract art at school and it inspired him.

He's one of a kind is my mate Bilal.

Anyway, it turned out in the end that it didn't matter what a mongoose was because the farm that Dad had used all our money to buy didn't even exist.

It was a **SCAM**.

And now we had ...

NO MONEY,

NO HOLIDAY

(and **NO MONGOOSE FARM**).

Dad explained that he'd bought the farm (which turned out to be **FAKE**) from the new guy at work (who mysteriously disappeared as soon as Dad handed over the cash). And that no one (not even the police) have been able to track him down since.

To be honest, I don't know how hard the police are looking, because when Mum phoned 999 and the police showed up at our flat I don't think they actually believed Dad.

They kept asking us if this was a joke and why someone would hand over their life savings to a guy they'd just met – **AND** they kept asking Dad what a mongoose farm was.

Dad explained that we now owned a plot of land in Wales with nothing on it.

Dad actually drove us all there for a camping trip a couple of weeks ago when we found out about the scam.

He said it could be our holiday home.

Mum pointed out that there was no house or caravan or even a toilet.

But Dad said we could create our own camping site.

It was actually quite fun for a while. We played cards and toasted marshmallows.

Then it got cold and the fire went out and Dad couldn't relight it and we didn't have any money to go to a restaurant so we had to eat cold beans out of a can and share a small tent

with Baby Angel who snored the whole night!

Anyway, Dad tried to explain to the police what a mongoose was. But the truth was that Baby Angel's crayon drawings would have been more useful.

And that's when Mum yelled, **"YOU'RE A MONGOOSE, PATRICK!"**

That's about the time the police left and Mum took Baby Angel and went to stay at Aunty Gemma's house for the night because she said she couldn't even look at Dad.

And I went up to my room and googled "mongoose" because I had absolutely no idea what one was. Here is what a mongoose looks like if you're interested:

So anyway ... back to the stew.

If Mum hadn't made this particularly disgusting stew, I never would have gone and sat with Dad in the living room.

And I never would have been forced to watch what he was watching on TV.

So I will be forever grateful for that stew.

Because what Dad was watching changed my **LIFE**.

DIARY OF A FUTURE BILLIONAIRE
THE TANK

So, yeah.

I was watching TV with Dad, trying not to choke to death on Mum's stew, when suddenly the screen turned black and this really intense music came on.

Dad sat up straight and turned the volume up.

Suddenly the words "**THIS IS A TRUE STORY**" flashed across the screen.

"What's this?" I asked Dad.

I'd forgotten that I wasn't supposed to be talking to him.

But Dad didn't answer. It was like he couldn't hear me. He was just staring at the screen.

Then this flashed up:

I'm a billionaire. I'm the best. I will show you my journey.

Next, there was an **EXPLOSION** on screen

and this huge guy with a giant moustache and a curly mullet appeared wearing a wrestling outfit. Then he ripped off his T-shirt and walked through the fire like something out of an action movie and said:

"**I'M THE TANK**."

The TV audience were chanting, "**TANK! TANK! TANK!**"

The Tank walked closer to the camera.

"I used to be just like you," he said, "and now I'm a billionaire. And I'm going to show you how I did it."

My mouth dropped open.

I mean, this guy looked serious.

He was a **BILLIONAIRE** and he was going to show other people how to become billionaires too!

Besides the fact it would be cool to get rich and make up for my dad's big mistake, who wouldn't want to be a billionaire and be able to buy anything?!

Like a huge mansion with a basketball court and a swimming pool and a four-screen cinema with a person who lives inside so they can serve you popcorn and hot dogs whenever you want.

Oh! And a pizza place in your own garden so you can go out for pizza every night if you want (and dessert!) and you don't have to pay because it's your restaurant.

But most of all I wanted the mansion so I could pick the bedroom furthest away from my baby sister's room because, as I mentioned, she has a serious snoring problem.

I haven't slept for almost two years.

Mum says that I'm **EXAGGERATING**, but I'm not! You can hear everything through the walls in our flat.

But this was soon to be a problem of the past.

Because I was going to be so rich that I'd probably live in my own mansion next door to Mum and Dad's mansion.

Then they'd have to phone me if they wanted to ask me a question like "Do you want some peanut butter on toast before bed?" And I'd say, "Yeah, four slices, please. Just get the butler to bring it over."

Anyway back to **THE TANK!**

After those words flashed across the screen that night, I became **OBSESSED** with the most amazing person ever.

The Tank used to have zero money and was pretty much homeless until one day he decided to become a billionaire.

I couldn't take my eyes off the screen!

It was the most brilliant thing I'd ever seen in my life!

And the best thing about it was that the Tank was just a **NORMAL** person.

He even grew up in Dundee, where we live!

"I can't believe he's from here!" I said, looking up at Dad.

"Yeah, I know," said Dad, keeping his eyes fixed on the screen. "He lived on my street when we were kids."

WHAT?!

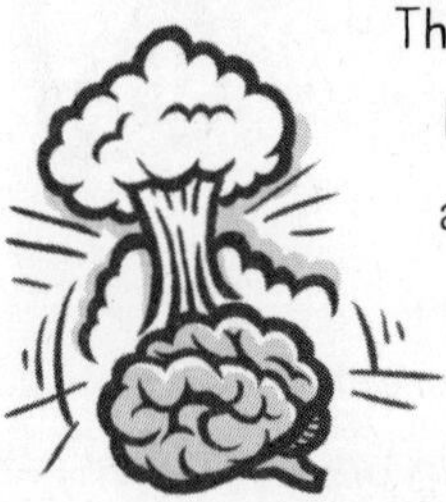

This was blowing my mind.

Dad had lived in the **SAME STREET** as a billionaire.

Dad turned the volume up again with the remote.

I didn't want to miss a thing!

The Tank was explaining how, first of all, he joined a wrestling club and trained hard every day until he became a professional **WRESTLER** and then eventually a world champion.

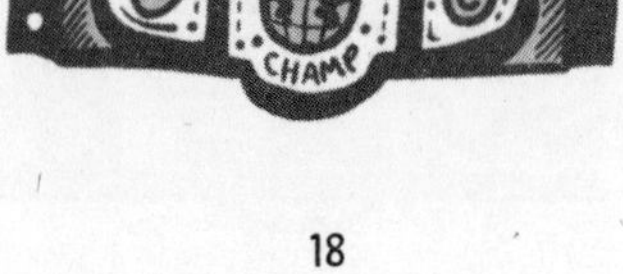

He got paid a lot and bought a huge house and a really cool car.

But the Tank said he still had a **FIRE IN HIS BELLY**.

He wanted more.

He wanted to become a **FILM STAR**.

So he did.

Then he wanted to become a billionaire **BUSINESSMAN**.

So he did.

Can you believe that?!

But it gets **BETTER**.

The Tank didn't just tell his story.

He gave advice about how to become **RICH** like him!

And at the end he pointed right down the camera and said: "If I can do it, then so can **YOU**."

I felt like he was looking through the TV right into my living room.

I've never felt anything like it.

It was like he was speaking directly to **ME**.

That's when I knew what I had to do.

I was going to do every single thing the Tank did and become the **WORLD'S YOUNGEST BILLIONAIRE!**

OK, so I don't think I'm going to be able to do exactly what the Tank did. But the day after I discovered him, I convinced our PE teacher Miss Nord to let us try **WRESTLING**, because if I was going to become the second-best wrestler to the Tank I needed to get going. Plus, if I was really good, maybe I wouldn't even have to go to maths any more. I would be pulled out of school and put straight into the ring.

The plan was for me to pick the **BEST** wrestlers in the class, then we could start a school wrestling team (with me as the star) and **WIN** national competitions. Just like the Tank had.

But it didn't go as planned.

Miss Nord said I could be one of the team captains and pick my team first since it was my idea.

Kallan was the other team captain.

I looked at my classmates.

They were all staring at me in that "**PICK ME! PICK ME!**" way.

I'd never felt so powerful.

I scanned the line, looking for the strongest, most fierce wrestler-in-the-making.

I spotted Bilal.

I guess you could call Bilal **UNIQUE**.

(And you could actually call him unique. Like to his face. And he'd just nod and smile because he obviously likes being jazzy.)

For example, Bilal wears fluorescent socks to school.

He wears a normal grey uniform, like everyone else. But instead of wearing grey socks, like our head teacher, Mr Ferrier, says we're supposed to, Bilal refuses and wears bright pink every day.

That's just Bilal.

Some kids at school call Bilal weird.

But, like I said, he's unique.

He was grinning at me.

This was a problem.

I mean, Bilal's my **BEST MATE**. But he's also the smallest person in our year.

April May was standing next to Bilal with her arms crossed. Her arm muscles were bulging. She was obviously the right choice.

I looked back at Bilal's tiny smiling face.

"Um, Bilal," I said.

Bilal grinned and did a bit of a swagger-walk over to me, his pink socks poppin'.

"Cheers, mate," he said. "I think that's the only time I've ever been picked first!"

"No worries," I said.

I'd pick April May next and all would be well.

"April May!" Kallan yelled, and winked at me. Kallan is a real **SHOW-OFF**.

I watched as April May walked over and stood beside Kallan.

"Miss! You said I could pick my team **FIRST**!" I shouted.

"Not your whole team," said Miss Nord. "That wouldn't be very fair, would it?"

I looked at Kallan.

"Your turn," he said, smirking.

Kallen really gets on my nerves. I've no idea why he enjoys winding me up so much. But he just does. Last week he kicked the back of my chair on the coach the whole way back after our school trip.

I looked at the rest of the class.

I felt **UNDER PRESSURE** - and I'm not good at making decisions under pressure!

Like the time I panicked and picked the shirt with pandas all over it to wear to the school disco because Baby Angel was screaming the entire supermarket down and Mum said we had to get out quick.

I turned to Bilal.

"You choose," I said.

Bilal nodded and yelled, "Mike!"

I gawked at Bilal. What was he thinking?! Mike was even **SKINNIER** than me!

"Rose," said Kallan.

Rose joined Kallan's team and gave April May a high five. Good choice.

Rose was fast. She won every race at the last sports day. No chance of getting her in a headlock.

I looked at the rest of the class.

I was just about to choose Radeen when Bilal shouted, "Luisa!"

I stared at him with my mouth wide open. "I didn't mean for you to pick the whole team!"

"Oh. Sorry," said Bilal.

I force-smiled at Luisa as she walked over to join us.

She scowled back at me.

She obviously didn't want to be in our team. And I knew that she hated PE because it made her hair go all frizzy.

I had no idea why Bilal had chosen her!

Kallan picked Tony next, so I got to pick Radeen. He was pretty good at sports.

Then I watched in horror as Radeen walked towards us with a slight **LIMP**.

"Hurt my knee playing football earlier," he said. "But I'll be fine."

I looked at Kallan and he

laughed. He'd known about Radeen's football injury. I needed to pay better attention if I was going to be successful!

After Kallan picked Nadia, Miss Nord said the rest of the class would watch and be tagged in when needed. Then she started demonstrating some wrestling moves she wanted us to try.

I decided to put Mike forward first.

He was up against Rose.

She **FLOORED** him hard in four seconds flat and Miss Nord sent him off to be checked by the nurse, just to be safe.

This was going to be more difficult than I thought.

Kallan put Tony in next.

I looked at Bilal, but he shook his head.

He clearly didn't want to go next after seeing the carnage with Mike. I didn't blame him. Tony was a big guy!

"Put me in," said Radeen. "I can take Tony."

Everyone watched as Tony tried to get Radeen into a hold position, like Miss Nord had shown us. But Radeen just kept ducking and dodging away at the last second.

Suddenly Radeen grabbed Tony and **SLAMMED** him down

on to the mat. Radeen pinned him there until Miss Nord blew her whistle.

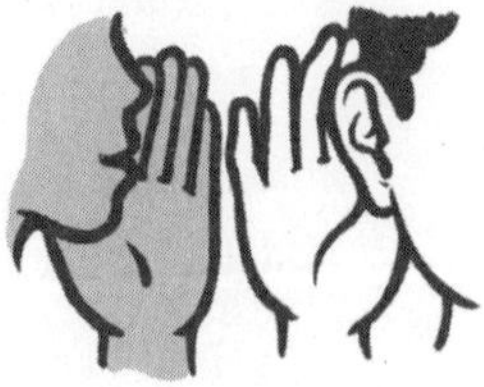

"Best out of three!" Miss Nord yelled.

Kallen moved forward and whispered something in Tony's ear, and Tony nodded.

Miss Nord blew her whistle again and, before Radeen could move out the way, Tony lunged at his left leg. Radeen yelled and clutched his knee and went down like a ton of bricks.

It was a dirty trick.

And it was obviously Kallan who was behind it.

Bilal went next. He was up against April May.

The second Miss Nord blew her whistle, I regretted not putting him in against Tony.

We all gasped as April May picked Bilal up and actually **LIFTED** him into the air, then spun him round a bit before slamming him down on the mat.

That wasn't even a move Miss Nord had shown us!

"Excellent, April May!" yelled Miss Nord.

April May smiled and put her hand out to help Bilal up, but he could hardly lift his arm. April May bent down and picked him up with both arms.

"You OK?" she asked.

Bilal nodded that he was.

April May stood him up and patted him on the shoulder.

"**ROUND TWO!**" cried Miss Nord.

Bilal turned and stared at me.

I've never seen a person look so scared. Thankfully, it was over fast.

April May floored Bilal quickly (after he tried to make a run for it), then carried him off to the side to recover.

"Thanks," gasped Bilal as April May lay him down on the bench.

"No worries. Good match," she said, shaking Bilal's limp arm. Then she ran back to her team.

"You all right?" I asked Bilal.

Bilal shook his head. "I can't feel my face. Is that bad?"

Miss Nord blew her whistle before I could answer.

That's when Bilal's eyes went wide and he whispered, "Luisa is our **SECRET WEAPON**. Put her in."

I wondered if Bilal had hit his head, because that made zero sense.

But then he grabbed my T-shirt and pulled me down towards him and said:

I figured that either he had a plan or he was seriously injured. I decided to respect his last wishes, just in case.

"Luisa, you're up!" I said.

Luisa looked at me like she wanted to kill me, then smoothed down her hair.

I hoped she took that fierce energy into the ring.

"Come on, Luisa – let's go," said Miss Nord, clapping her hands.

This was going to be brutal.

Luisa stood there, rolling her eyes, as Miss Nord blew her whistle.

Nadia rushed forward and tried to put Luisa in a headlock, and Luisa yelled, "Get off my hair!"

And that's when Luisa totally lost it. She slipped out of the headlock and did one of the moves Miss Nord had showed us and floored Nadia! (And I'm pretty sure I heard her growl when she did it.)

We all stood there, stunned, as Luisa held Nadia down with one hand and used her other hand to re-smooth her hair.

I turned to Bilal.

He smiled and winked at me. He **KNEW** that would happen. He knew Luisa's hair would get messed up and she would get **THE RAGE**.

He was a genius.

"Well done, Luisa!" yelled Miss Nord. "OK, the captains are up next!"

I took a deep breath and started jogging on the spot. Just like I'd seen the Tank do on TV.

I looked at Kallan.

He was doing the same.

This obviously wasn't his first wrestling match. But it **WAS** mine.

The Tank says:

WINNING IS A MINDSET. IF YOU CAN SEE IT, IT CAN HAPPEN. IF YOU BELIEVE IT ... IT WILL HAPPEN.

In that moment, I could **SEE** it.

And I **BELIEVED** it.

I was going to **WIN**.

I faced Kallan and took a deep breath.

The whistle blew.

I ducked into a crouching position, bracing myself for attack.

Kallan was staring at me while he moved really fast from side to side, like a weird crab.

I watched him scuttle about. There was something familiar about the way he was moving. I'd seen it before.

I gasped.

It was the Tank. This was one of his **SIGNATURE MOVES**.

He'd used it when he'd won his first world champion title in Las Vegas.

I knew this wasn't a coincidence. Kallan had also watched the documentary last night.

Then Kallen dropped to the floor and tried to grab my legs. Just like the Tank had done in Las Vegas.

But I'd already jumped into the air and leapt clear over him.

Like a **NINJA**.

I'd watched the documentary too.

Everyone gasped.

Kallan scrambled to his feet and narrowed his eyes.

I smiled at him.

"**TIME TO FLY OR TIME TO DIE. AND I'M GOING TO FLY**," I said. (Because that's something else the Tank says.)

I could tell that no one else knew what was going on because they were all looking at each other and shrugging.

Kallan and I wrestled for a bit, but I couldn't get him pinned.

That's when I remembered something else the Tank said: "**BE UNPREDICTABLE**."

I lay down on the mat like a starfish. Completely still.

Ha! Kallan hadn't been expecting **THAT**, had he?!

Suddenly Kallan threw himself on top of me and pinned my arms down.

Miss Nord blew her whistle, and Kallan leant over and whispered in my ear, "**ALWAYS REMEMBER MY GREATNESS.**"

Miss Nord announced the final round.

Kallan **RAN** full force at me with his arms outstretched.

Oh no. This was the Tank's number-one move.

It was all over pretty fast.

I don't really remember much. But I do remember Bilal standing over me and I think he was praying, so it must have looked bad.

I should have known **THEN** that Kallan was going to be a problem.

Needless to say, I won't be the next wrestling champion.

I needed a new plan.

I was feeling pretty defeated when I got home. Then I saw something sitting on the doorstep.

It was the Tank!

Not the **ACTUAL** Tank, obviously. But there was a book on the doorstep with his face on the front cover.

I dropped my bag and picked it up:

HOW TO WIN AT EVERYTHING: THE ONLY AUTOBIOGRAPHY YOU WILL NEED by the Tank.

There was a Post-it note inside. It said:

I looked around.

I had no idea how the book had got there. It was just sitting on the doorstep, waiting for me to get home!

It was fate.

A miracle.

I started to wonder if the Tank **HAD** been speaking directly to me last night through the TV. Had **HE** sent the book to me?

None of it made sense, but I took it as a pretty big sign that the universe was telling me to become a billionaire.

I gasped as I opened the book.

It was a **SIGNED** copy.

And it was dedicated to **ME**.

My heart was racing.

Well. It didn't say my name exactly but it **DID** say:

Never let failure get in your way. You can do this.

Somehow the Tank knew what had happened at school today and he'd sent me a message to keep going.

This was the most amazing thing that had ever happened to me!

I ran up to my bedroom and put a sign on my door:

I couldn't be disturbed.

This was **TOO BIG**.

I turned the page and read:

SIX STEPS TO BECOMING A BILLIONAIRE

I gasped again.

There were actual steps.

Steps to becoming a billionaire...

STEP ONE: JOIN THE 5 A.M. CLUB
STEP TWO: A BILLION-POUND BUSINESS IDEA
STEP THREE: FIND A MONEY GUY
STEP FOUR: EXPAND YOUR BUSINESS
STEP FIVE: BE A BILLIONAIRE

It was so simple! Why didn't **EVERYONE** just do this?

I couldn't answer for everyone in the world. But I could answer for me.

I was going to follow the steps.

Every.

Single.

One.

STEP ONE:
JOIN THE 5 A.M. CLUB

I stayed up all night.

I had to.

I couldn't sleep until I'd read every single word.

(I also couldn't sleep because Baby Angel's snoring was hitting new levels of **OUT OF CONTROL**.)

I finished the book at 4.30 a.m. and decided to go to sleep for half an hour to get my beauty sleep, because Step One was:

JOIN THE 5 A.M. CLUB

THE EARLY BIRD CATCHES THE WORM. THE LAZY BIRD STAYS IN BED WHILE THE OTHER BIRDS EAT ALL THE WORMS. SO GET UP EARLY AND CATCH SOME WORMS!!

Which meant I had to get up at 5 a.m. from now on because the Tank said that's what billionaires do.

When my alarm went off on Wednesday morning, I had NO IDEA what was going on.

I mean, it was DARK outside for a start.

I almost pulled the covers over my head and went back to sleep.

But then I remembered about the worms.

Or rather, the cash.

I wanted the cash.

I wanted **ALL** the cash!

So I pulled myself out of bed and headed into the hall.

It was dark and everyone else was still asleep (even though Baby Angel was snoring the house down!).

I switched a lamp on.

This felt **WEIRD**. I was up and awake in the house by myself.

I wasn't exactly sure what I was supposed to do between 5 a.m. and 8.30 a.m. so I went to get some breakfast.

I made myself a bowl of cereal, then sat down and looked at all the junk mail on the kitchen table.

That was when I saw it.

My first **BUSINESS OPPORTUNITY**!

It was a leaflet with loads of dogs on the front and the words:

I called the number on the leaflet right away.

It rang for ages until eventually someone answered: "Um, what? Hello? Is everything OK?"

So that's when I said that everything was OK.

Actually, it was **BETTER** than OK.

"I'm calling because I just saw your leaflet and I wanted to let you know I can help urgently!"

There was a pause on the other end for a moment.

"Is this a joke?"

"NO," I said. "It's not a joke. I just saw your leaflet and I wanted to let you know I'm available to walk dogs right away!"

The lady on the other end sighed.

"It's the middle of the night," she said. "I thought this was urgent!"

So that's when I explained that it was actually 5.15 a.m. and that it just **LOOKED** like night because it wasn't quite light outside yet.

"Early bird catches the worm!" I told her.

She didn't say anything for a while.

"Meet me at Slesser Park at half seven," she said at last.

"Okey-doke!"

Then she hung up.

I couldn't believe it.

I couldn't believe I'd just got a **JOB**!

I'd learn the ropes, then branch out and start my **OWN** dog-walking business by the end of the week!

I had a shower and started to put my school clothes on when I realized something.

I was a **PROFESSIONAL DOG WALKER** now.

I stopped.

What did professional dog walkers wear?

I assumed they wore sporty stuff for running around the park with the dogs. They also probably wore dog-related stuff too, because they all loved dogs.

I made a mental note to order a T-shirt online with a

photo of a dog and the name of my dog-walking business on it.

Actually, I'd get two T-shirts because I planned on being pretty successful **FAST**, which meant I'd probably have to bring someone on to help me ASAP.

I thought hard.

Did I have any clothes with dogs on them?

Then all of a sudden my brain pinged into action. (I swear getting up at 5 a.m. really was helping my brain work better!)

Dad had got Mum a pair of pug pyjamas for Christmas because Mum loves dogs.

I decided I would wear shorts, trainers and Mum's pug pyjama top. It looked like a regular T-shirt.

I tiptoed into Mum and Dad's room.

Mum was sprawled out in the bed by herself (which meant Dad must still be sleeping on the couch).

I gently opened a drawer.

Baby Angel woke up and stood up in her cot.

Her eyes were closed.

Oh, God.

She was doing her **SCARY BABY** thing again!

She does this thing where she wakes up and stands up straight in her cot while she's still asleep. It's like baby sleepwalking. Except she doesn't walk. She just stands (so I guess you could call it **SLEEP-STANDING**).

Anyway, it's super creepy!

"**POOPY. POOPY NOW**," she said.

Oh no.

She was going to poop her nappy!

I knew that as soon as she did that she would start crying and wake Mum up.

I rushed over and checked her nappy.

Empty.

She must have just been dreaming. Phew!

I gently lay her back down and stroked her head for a few minutes. She sounded like a dinosaur, but she looked super cute. I tucked her in and tiptoed back to Mum's dresser.

It was hard to see in the dark, but I eventually spotted the pug pyjama top.

I grabbed it and put it on over my long-sleeved top and got out quickly before Baby Angel woke up again.

I wrote a note for Mum saying I'd had my breakfast and had left early for school (which wasn't actually lying).

The park was right next to my house, so that was a bonus.

I made sure I was there **EIGHT MINUTES EARLY** because the Tank says:

MAKE SURE YOU'RE EARLY BUT NOT TOO EARLY. FIVE MINUTES ISN'T ENOUGH TIME TO DEAL WITH THE UNEXPECTED, BUT TEN MINUTES MAKES YOU SEEM TOO KEEN. DON'T LOOK DESPERADO!

At exactly 7.30 a.m. a lady with a tiny dog walked into the park.

I rushed over.

"Hello," I said. "I'm Ben. Are you here for my professional dog-walking services?"

The lady looked me up and down and then stared at my T-shirt.

"Um, no thank you," she said.

And then she hurried off.

"Are you Ben?" said a voice from behind me.

I turned round and saw the **BIGGEST** dog I had ever seen in real life.

"I'm Gael," she said. "This is Terrance."

"Ben!" I said confidently, and then offered her my hand to shake.

The lady was also staring at my T-shirt (I guess it looked a bit pyjama-y), but she took my hand and shook it. I squeezed hers as hard as I could at the same time, because the Tank says, "You need to develop a **STRONG POWER HANDSHAKE** so people will know you mean business!"

"Ouch!" cried the woman.

I let go.

"You almost broke my hand!" she yelled, dropping the lead and holding her hand carefully with her other one.

I looked down at the dog lead lying on the grass.

And then at Terrance.

All of a sudden, Terrance **RAN**.

"Get him!" the lady yelled.

I chased Terrance, but he was fast.

Too fast.

I saw him stop to smell a wee that another dog had done on a tree, so I took that opportunity and dived across the grass towards his lead.

But he ran off as soon as I hit the ground.

I was starting to panic now. If I didn't catch this dog, I'd lose the job!

I got up and looked around.

Terrance had **DISAPPEARED**.

This was bad.

Suddenly I heard a scream coming from the other side of the park. I turned and saw Terrance running away from the lady with the tiny dog.

I rushed over.

"That dog almost **KNOCKED** me over!" she screamed.

"**I'M SO SORRY!**" I yelled behind me.

I ran after Terrance.

He was heading for the pond.

This was **REALLY** bad.

There were swans in that pond.

I watched as Terrance leapt into the water and started swimming towards the swans.

"**TERRANCE!**" I shouted.

Gael appeared beside me.

"Get him!" she cried. "Before he attacks those swans!"

I didn't have time to think. I **JUMPED** in. Trainers and all.

It turned out the pool was quite shallow and I could stand.

Terrance turned round when he saw me wading over. He swam towards me, barking happily.

I pulled him out of the pond. He knocked me down and sat on top of me and licked my face.

"Good," said Gael, putting his lead into my soaking wet hand. "He likes you. Don't let him off his lead, **UNDERSTAND**?"

I pushed Terrance off me, then sat up and nodded.

"I was going to stay and show you the ropes, but I need to go and get my hand checked now!"

"I'm so sorry," I said. "I didn't mean to break your hand. I just—"

Gael cut me off. "The other dogs will be here in five minutes. That's the meeting point," she said, pointing to the dog-poop bin next to the exit. "My husband will bring the dogs to you and meet you back at the meeting place at 8.45 a.m. sharp. OK? If the dogs are still alive and in one piece at 8.45 a.m., I'll give you **£7** per dog."

I beamed.

She turned to leave, then suddenly stopped and said to me, "You **CAN** handle this, right?"

I pushed Terrance out of the way and stood up straight.

"Yes. **YES, I CAN**," I said, wiping the pondwater off my forehead. "I'm a professional dog walker."

The lady nodded and rushed off, clutching her hand.

I waited with Terrance at the dog-poop bin next to the gates and at exactly 7.55 a.m. a van with the words **PUP PALACE** on the side pulled up.

A man got out and handed me four dogs.

"I see you've got **TERRANCE THE TERRIBLE** today!" he said, laughing.

The man showed me how to operate the special dog-walking lead which meant I could walk loads of dogs at once.

"I suggest you take the four little ones in one hand and

keep your strongest hand free for Terrance."

I nodded and watched the man demonstrate how the dog-walking lead worked.

"Whatever you do, **DON'T** press this button. It releases all the leads from the main section."

I nodded.

"You been swimming?" he asked.

"Um ... sort of," I replied.

"See you back here at 8.45 a.m. Give them a good workout, OK?"

I nodded and the man left.

I was in charge of five dogs. This was a lot of responsibility. But it also meant I was about to get paid a lot of **MONEY**!

I was going to get **£35** for **ONE HOUR** of dog walking!

"OK, guys," I said to the dogs. "Let's go for a light jog, shall we?"

My plan was to tire them out. Especially Terrance.

This was going to be easy, I thought.

I wondered how many dogs I'd be able to handle by myself when I started my own business next week. *Probably around ten*, I thought.

I did the calculations in my head as I jogged.

Gael was paying me **£35** an hour. If I did this every day, by the end of the week I'd have made over **£200**.

Then I'd launch my own business. I'd keep it local to begin with, but then I'd take on some staff and offer our services at **ALL** the parks in our town! We were going to be **HUGE**.

The dogs started to overtake me.

It was fine at first. They just sort of pulled me along with their leads, which made jogging easier.

Then Terrance spotted a football and started barking.

Then **ALL** the dogs **BOLTED** towards the football pitch and pulled me along with them.

I had to run faster than I've ever run before, just to avoid being dragged along the grass!

But then I tripped...

I must have accidently pressed the release button as I fell because **ALL** their leads dropped to the ground and the little dogs went running off in different directions.

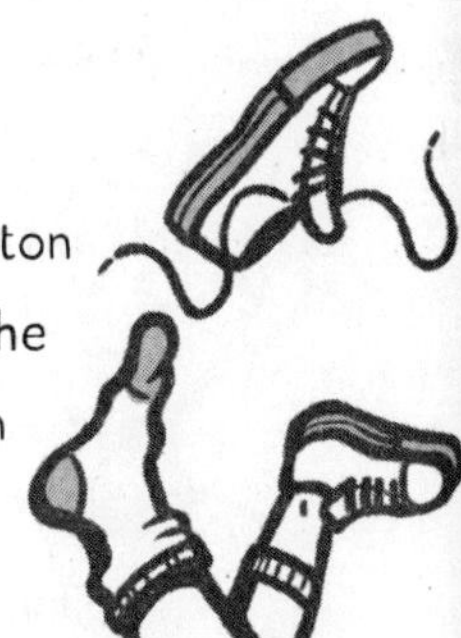

Terrance was destroying the football he'd been chasing and a group of men were shouting at me to "**COME AND DEAL WITH THIS!**"

It was an epic disaster.

I ran over to them and secured Terrance with the help of the football guys. I handed them back their slobbery ball and apologized.

But I still had four dogs running loose!

I couldn't catch them all by myself.

I needed help!

I took my phone out of my pocket and called Bilal.

"S'up?" Bilal answered.

"**PARK. NOW. BRING TREATS!**"

That's all I could get out. I was completely out of breath!

Two minutes later, Bilal came running into the park.

He looked shocked when he saw the state of me.

"**TREATS!**" I yelled.

Bilal handed me a box of Maltesers. "That's all I could find in the house," he said. "What's happening? Why are you soaking wet?!"

I still couldn't speak in full sentences. "Dog walking. Four little ones on the loose. Can't find them."

The great thing about having someone like Bilal as your best mate is that he thinks outside the box himself, so he never questions my life choices.

"Do you mean those dogs in the sandpit?" asked Bilal, pointing behind me.

It was them!

We rushed over. The dogs spotted us and were just about to make a run for it, but I shook the box of Maltesers and they came running to us.

IT WORKED!

Bilal gave them each a Malteser as I secured their leads.

"Are you going to clean that up?" a woman shouted at us, pointing.

One of the dogs had done a **POO** on top of a sandcastle.

The child next to it was crying.

"Disgusting!" the woman said. "My child is probably **TRAUMATIZED** now!"

The lady picked up her screaming, traumatized child and stormed off.

That's when I realized that Gael hadn't given me any poo bags!

I guess she assumed I'd have my own, because she thought I was a professional dog walker!

I looked around for something to pick it up with.

Terrance started barking loudly as the little dogs ate their Maltesers.

"You'd better give him one too," I said. "Or he might freak out again!"

So Bilal opened the box and Terrance stuck his head right in.

"You shouldn't do that, you know!" said a man, walking past. "Chocolate is **POISONOUS** to dogs!"

I gasped and looked at Bilal.

We'd given them chocolate!

ALL of them.

I started to panic.

We'd just **POISONED FIVE DOGS**!

I definitely wasn't getting paid now. And I'd probably get sued, and my new dog-walking business would go bust before it even started.

"We need to get them to a vet!" I yelled. "Now!"

"How?" said Bilal. "It's on the other side of town!"

"A taxi!" I shouted.

We called a taxi on my phone and it arrived right away.

But as soon as the taxi guy saw the dogs, he shook his head and drove off.

"**THESE DOGS ARE DYING!**" I screamed after him.

"Look!" said Bilal. "The bus!"

The bus had stopped along the street.

We held the leads tight and ran. We caught the bus just as it was about to leave.

"Do you stop near the vet?" I shout-asked.

The bus driver nodded. "But you're not bringing all those dogs on this bus!"

"We have to!" I yelled. "It's an emergency!"

The bus driver shook his head.

At this point I almost burst into tears.

"Sir, these dogs have been **POISONED** at the park and we have to get them to a vet **NOW** or they'll **DIE**. Please!"

But the bus driver kept shaking his head.

That's when an old woman shouted down the bus: "For the love of God, **LET THEM ON**!"

The driver let us on.

It was only three stops to the vet, which was lucky, because we didn't know how much time these dogs had left!

We rushed inside and explained that all the dogs had been **POISONED AT THE PARK**, then loads of nurses came rushing out and took the dogs into the back.

Bilal and I collapsed into the waiting seats.

After a few minutes, the vet came out and asked us to step into a side room.

I looked at Bilal. They wouldn't ask you to step into a side room unless something was very wrong.

This was it.

The dogs were dead.

All of them.

We were **DOG MURDERERS**!

The vet asked us to have a seat and told us that she needed to get as much information about the poison the dogs had ingested as possible.

We nodded.

"We brought it with us," said Bilal.

Bilal took the Maltesers box out of his bag and placed it on the table in front of the vet.

The vet looked surprised. "Is the poisonous substance inside that box?"

We watched as she got up and put on some goggles and gloves.

Then she opened the box.

A **TERRIBLE** smell came out.

The vet stared at us. "Is this a Maltesers box with a small dog poo inside?"

"That's exactly what it is," said Bilal.

Bilal turned to me. "I picked up the poo with the box before we left. I didn't know what else to do. I didn't want

us to get fined for leaving it on top of a sandcastle!"

The vet looked very confused.

"What exactly did the dogs ingest?" she asked.

"Maltesers," I said.

"OK. How many Maltesers?"

I looked at Bilal.

This was **BAD**.

"One each," said Bilal. "But the big one..." His eyes flicked to me. "He ate **TWO**."

The vet closed the lid of the Maltesers box and took her goggles off.

"I'll be back in a moment," she said.

We sat there **SWEATING** in a hot room that smelled like dog poo for what felt like a lifetime until the vet eventually appeared again.

"I have good news and bad news. Although chocolate is not good for dogs, a small amount, like the amount ingested today, is unlikely to do any serious harm. I've examined all the dogs and will keep them here today for observation, just in case."

I've never been more **RELIEVED** in my life!

I looked at Bilal.

We **WEREN'T** dog murderers!

We weren't going to jail!

"What's the bad news?" said Bilal.

That's when the vet told us that the receptionist had called the phone number on each of their collars to alert their owners of the suspected poisoning and that they were all on their way.

"However," she said, "it looks like Terrance will be staying to have a procedure with us. We discovered something rather serious during our examination and contacted his owner. He isn't a patient of ours – in fact, I'm not sure he's seen a vet in a while – but they've agreed to let us go ahead and operate. You bringing him here today might just have saved his life."

This was a lot to take in.

We hadn't murdered five dogs.

In fact, we had maybe **SAVED ONE DOG'S LIFE**.

I was riding the high of not being a dog murderer when suddenly there was a furious knock at the door.

The vet got up and opened it – and that's when I saw Gael.

Oh no.

Her arm was in a sling thing and she looked pretty angry.

Thankfully the vet asked to talk to her outside.

We could hear Gael shouting about being put out of business in one day and having to cover her clients' vet bills.

But then we heard the vet say, "They are clearly **SCHOOLCHILDREN**. You should not have put them in charge of all those dogs **UNSUPERVISED**."

Gael went quiet and after a few moments the vet came back in and said we were free to go.

Gael was nowhere to be seen when we walked out.

"Can we see Terrance before we go?" I asked hopefully.

The vet smiled and led us up the corridor.

"He's just being prepped for surgery. But you can see him through the glass window. Don't worry – I expect him to make a full recovery."

I knocked gently on the glass and Terrance looked at me and started wagging his tail.

"**GOOD LUCK, BOY!**"

I whispered.

That afternoon when I got home from school, Mum was sitting on the sofa, furiously typing away on her laptop.

She snapped it shut when I walked in.

"Where were you this morning?" she said, getting up to give me a hug. "You left early and then I got a message from **SCHOOL** to say you'd arrived fifteen minutes late!" She stared at me.

"Oh, um. Sorry!" I said. "I went jogging in the park ... with Bilal," I added, so she didn't worry. "We lost track of time. It was, um, to raise money for a dog-charity thing!"

"Well, I'm glad you wanted to help the charity, but you definitely can't lose track of time like that, Ben. You can't be late for school!"

"I know," I said. "I'm really sorry. It was an accident. It won't happen again."

Mum nodded, then she asked, "Will you be going again tomorrow?"

"Um ... I don't think so," I said.

There was no way I could go near the park **EVER** again. Gael would probably kill me **ON SIGHT**.

I sat down next to Mum.

"How's the writing?" I asked, changing the subject.

Mum stared at me.

"What's that smell?" she said.

Oh no. She could smell the **DOGS** on me.

She'd be **FURIOUS** if she found out I'd almost murdered five dogs today and lied to her about where I'd been!

"Gaba!" Baby Angel yelled.

I leapt up.

"I'll get it!" I said, rescuing Baby Angel's dummy from the carpet. I gave it a wipe and popped it back into her mouth.

"What are you watching on TV?" I asked.

Baby Angel bounced up and down

on the cushion-den she had made on the living-room floor.

"**DINOHOR!**"

I pulled Baby Angel on to my knee and she snuggled up to me.

I know I'm too old for kids' programmes, but I swear this one is **AMAZING**!

Suddenly Baby Angel pulled her head away and gave me a look. She spat out her dummy.

"**YUCKY! BEN SMELL YUCKY!**" she yelled.

Mum came over and started sniffing me from head to toe.

She stopped at my toes.

"It's your trainers. They **STINK**, Ben!"

I'd had to keep them on all day to try to dry them out.

Just then Dad came in.

"Ben's trainers are stinking the flat out and we don't have money for a new pair!" Mum yelled at him.

Dad looked **SHOCKED**. I couldn't tell if it was because of the smell or because those were the most words Mum had said to him in almost two weeks.

He put down his work bag and smiled. "Don't worry. I'm on it," he said. "I actually just took on a **SECOND JOB** today!"

"Oh," said Mum. (She obviously wasn't expecting Dad to say that.)

Dad rushed to the kitchen and grabbed a takeaway pizza menu off the table.

"I'm going to **TREAT** you all to a takeaway **PIZZA** tonight from that new place that's opened down the street. No cooking!" he said, looking at Mum. "You just keep writing. I'll take care of dinner and the baby and everything!"

"**PIA!**" screamed Baby Angel.

She loved pizza.

I loved pizza too.

I mean, who **DOESN'T** love pizza?!

Dad handed me the menu and told me to order whatever I wanted!

I didn't need to see the menu. I knew exactly what I wanted.

I wanted an **EXTRA-LARGE CHEESE**.

"PIA!" yelled Baby Angel. She was drooling now.

I wiped her face with my sleeve and popped her dummy back in.

"You can share my pia," I said.

Baby Angel clapped her hands furiously.

The pizza was **DELICIOUS**.

Mum ate at the kitchen table, while still typing on her laptop. Dad fussed around her, bringing her napkins and water, and she even let him give her a quick kiss on the cheek.

Pizza made everyone happier!

But then suddenly Mum gasped.

She was holding the pizza menu in her hand.

"Patrick! It costs **£18** for a pizza! **£18** for a piece of **HOT BREAD WITH CHEESE** on it! We can't afford that! Who around here can?! What were you **THINKING**?"

"Um ... I didn't realize how pricey they were," said Dad.

"You are terrible with money, Patrick!" sighed Mum as she stormed out to the living room.

I sighed.

We were all going to be eating Mum's stew for the rest of our lives!

That's when it happened.

Like a light bulb going on in my head.

No ... like a light bulb exploding in my head!

I'd just had a **BRILLIANT BUSINESS IDEA**.

I was going to start a takeaway pizza business! A **CHEAP** takeaway pizza business!

And I was going to make it so cheap that people would be able to have takeaway pizza **EVERY NIGHT** if they wanted!

Then I'd take my business global and turn it into a cheap pizza **EMPIRE**.

The Tank was right.

Sometimes it's when you're at your lowest that you start

to win.

My dog-walking business might have failed.

But that didn't matter.

Because I was about to start a **PIZZA REVOLUTION**.

STEP THREE: FIND A MONEY GUY

As soon as I got to school the next day, I asked Bilal the most important question he'd ever be asked in his life:

"Do you want to be my **BUSINESS PARTNER**?"

He said yes.

When I first decided to become a billionaire, I thought I'd do it by myself. But yesterday's dog-walking disaster made me think about something I'd read in the Tank's autobiography:

NO ONE GETS TO THE TOP ALONE

hard work, determination (and my obvious natural talent!) then you're WRONG.

No one gets to the top alone. REMEMBER that. We all need HELP in our journey to the top. And there's ZERO SHAME in admitting that. Everyone brings a different talent to the table. So make sure your table is FULL of different types of talent you can feast on!

And most importantly ... make sure you get yourself a great MONEY GUY.

GOT IT?

A money guy? I knew who to pick. Me and Bilal do most things together, so it made sense to become billionaires together too.

And, to be honest with you, **MATHS** is probably my **WORST** subject at school (along with every other subject, according to my teacher, Mrs Knot).

Well, that's what my last report said anyway (Mum and Dad were NOT happy):

Bad at maths
Bad at creative writing
Bad at everything

(OK, so that's not **EXACTLY** what it said, but close enough.)

Mum was furious. At first I thought she was furious with Mrs Knot (because it hadn't been very nice of her to write all those things about me).

But then I realized that it was **ME** she was furious with!

She kept saying I spend too much time watching TV and that she wanted me to start creative writing like she did, so that I could unlock my creative-writing **POTENTIAL**.

That's when she gave me this writing pad (which has actually come in quite useful to record how I'm going to become a billionaire!).

Bilal was by far the best at maths in our class, so I knew that he would make a great **MONEY GUY**. We also lived in the same block of flats, which would make business meetings easier to arrange.

I waited until lunchtime to tell Bilal my business idea.

I thought it was **BRILLIANT**, but I was a little bit nervous about what Bilal would think.

I mean, if he didn't think it was a good idea, I would have no choice but to terminate him as my business partner. (And I was worried that might get in the way of our friendship.)

But I didn't have to worry for long.

"Cheap pizza! Bro! I am **IN**! Let's go to mine after school to crunch the numbers."

CRUNCH THE NUMBERS

That was exactly the sort of thing the Tank would say. Bilal was already talking like **THE TANK** and he hadn't even been introduced to his words of wisdom yet.

I was well up for going round to Bilal's, because it meant I would get something normal to eat and wouldn't have to listen to Mum shouting at Dad about the mongoose fiasco.

When we got there after school, Bilal wanted to know more about the Tank.

I told him that I'd tried to find the documentary online so I could watch it again (and again, again!) but it wasn't available yet as it was too new.

Bilal nodded, then opened his mum's laptop and found the documentary **IN FOUR SECONDS FLAT**.

I think he might actually be a genius.

We sat and watched the whole documentary. Bilal didn't say a word for a whole hour.

Then he turned to me and said, "That was **AMAZING**."

I grinned and nodded loads, because it was!

"I can't believe the Tank went from having **NOTHING** to becoming a **BILLIONAIRE** in only **THREE YEARS**!" he said. "That means we could be billionaires by the time we're teenagers!"

"And millionaires before that!" I added.

"Follow me! You need to show me your plan! Actually, wait. Let's go in here."

Then he led the way to the bedroom he shared with his big brother, Yusef.

I watched as Bilal took one of Yusef's posters off the wall to reveal a **HUGE TV SCREEN**.

I stared at it with my mouth wide open.

"Yusef doesn't want Mum to know he bought it," he explained. "He's supposed to be giving her all his wages from Tesco because she helped buy his car."

I stared at the huge screen.

I had no idea Tesco paid so well!

It didn't seem to when Mum worked there.

Bilal switched it on and handed me a stylus pen. "It works as a presentation screen too."

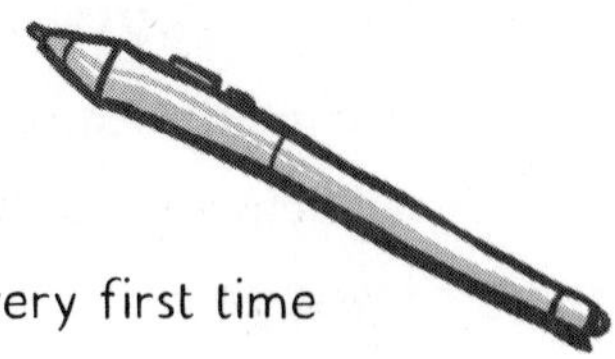

I took a deep breath and for the very first time I wrote out the name of our business:

CHEAPO PIZZA

Bilal said he thought it was the **BEST BUSINESS NAME** he'd ever heard.

He asked me how I came up with it, so I explained about the takeaway menu where the pizzas were **£18** and what Mum had said about that being too much for anyone around here. And how, even when we **DO** get a takeaway pizza, Mum forces everyone to "**EAT THEIR CRUSTS**" because it's expensive (even though I hate crusts, unless it's stuffed crust, but we never get that).

"Wait," interrupted Bilal. "We should only make **STUFFED CRUST** pizza."

"That would cost too much." I said.

Bilal closed his eyes for a second and then he opened them really wide and said, "Wait. So everyone hates the crust, right?"

I nodded.

"Then we **LOSE** the crust."

I thought for a second.

A completely **CRUSTLESS PIZZA**.

It was perfect.

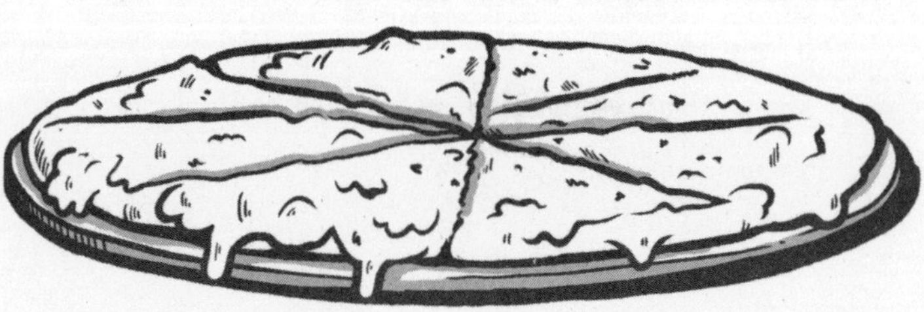

We would be giving our customers even more pizza for their money!

I grinned at Bilal.

THIS was the reason I'd chosen Bilal to be my business partner.

Because like the Tank says:

To be successful at business, you need to think outside the box or surround yourself with people who do.

Just like the Tank, Bilal always thinks **OUTSIDE THE BOX**.

I knew that if I was going to make it big I was going to need a unique mind.

And Bilal definitely had one of those.

"We can use my kitchen as **PIZZA CENTRAL**," said Bilal. "Mum's working nights this week. But we can't make a mess. She'd kill me."

As long as we cleaned everything up, no one would ever know that we were running a cheap takeaway pizza business (soon to become a 

) from Bilal's mum's kitchen.

The next step was to figure out how we were going to **DELIVER** the pizzas.

I said that if we could design something to secure the pizzas and keep them flat that I could deliver them on my bike.

Bilal said we could use kitchen foil to wrap the pizzas, so they didn't go cold, and make sure we re-used the foil each time to **SAVE MONEY**.

Things were going well.

We had a pizza kitchen, a delivery vehicle and a way to keep the pizzas hot until they were delivered.

After that, it was time to think about **ADVERTISING**.

Luckily, Bilal knew the code for the school printer because he was on the pupil council.

Bilal's role on the council meant that he got to help the teachers' and parents' council make big decisions about our school. Like, where we went on our school trips and what playground equipment we bought with our fundraising money. Last term, he even started a campaign that actually got rid of the cream of

fish soup we had at dinners for a while!

So he was quite a powerful person to have on board.

"We can print **TAKEAWAY LEAFLETS** in the school library tomorrow," Bilal said. "As long as we don't print too many, the librarian won't get suspicious."

It was all coming together!

This was actually going to **WORK**.

Until today, I had never used the ancient school printer before.

What happened was a **GENUINE** accident.

"What have you done?" said Bilal.

His eyes were wide.

I'd typed "**200**" instead of "20".

The printer was spewing out loads of **COLOUR** leaflets.

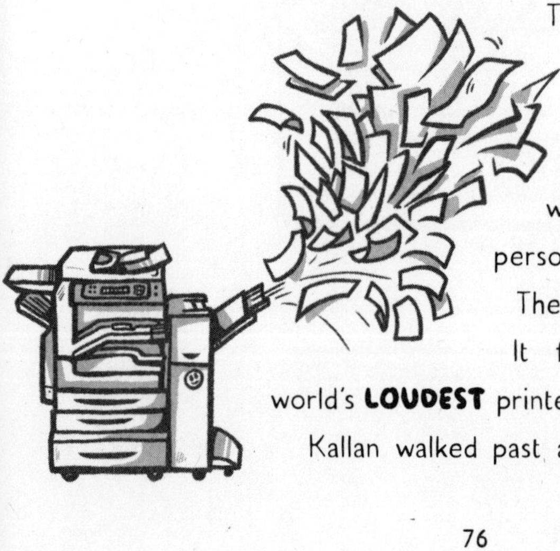

They looked great, but pupils weren't allowed to print in colour. They also weren't allowed to print personal documents.

The printer was going wild. It felt like it was the world's **LOUDEST** printer.

Kallan walked past and said he would tell

the teacher unless Bilal gave him the answers to the science quiz we had to take home. It was annoying, but Bilal has a photographic memory and was able to give Kallan the answers while we tried to get the printer to calm down.

Bilal was pressing "cancel" over and over again.

But the printer wouldn't stop.

It was like it was **POSSESSED**.

I wondered what would happen if I pulled the plug. Would the printer just keep going? **POWERED** by the Tank somehow? (I was beginning to feel like he was somehow watching me, guiding me.) He wouldn't want this business venture to fail, I was sure of it.

Suddenly the machine stopped.

The little screen flashed:

Bilal sighed with relief and began scooping up all the leaflets and stuffing them into his backpack.

And then we ran.

AFTER SCHOOL

When Dad got home from work, he called out that he had a big surprise for us.

And then he brought an absolutely **MASSIVE DOG** into the kitchen.

I couldn't believe it!

"**TERRANCE!**" I gasped.

"Well, if your mum likes that name, son…" said my dad.

"Whose dog is that?!" said Mum.

Dad stared at Mum with a huge grin on his face.

"He's **YOURS**, darling!" he said, throwing his hands in the air. "To apologize for everything."

Terrance barked loudly and leapt on top of me. He remembered me!

Baby Angel started screaming.

I laughed and gave Terrance a big hug.

"It's just a doggy!" I said to Baby Angel.

I held Terrance's big floppy ears up in the air.

"Look," I said. "Now he's a bunny rabbit!"

Baby Angel giggled.

I stuck my tongue out at her and then I gave her the dummy.

Mum looked like she was going to **EXPLODE**.

I'm only ten, but even I know that bringing a huge dog home without even asking Mum about it isn't a good idea.

"Patrick, please tell me you're joking," said Mum.

I could tell by the look on Dad's face that he definitely wasn't joking.

And I could tell by the look on Mum's face that Dad had just made everything worse.

"Patrick!" she screamed. "It's going to cost a **FORTUNE** to feed a dog like that! Look at the size of him. And are dogs even allowed in this building? What were you thinking?!"

Terrance barked loudly again and then jumped on to the sofa and started biting Baby Angel's favourite teddy bear.

Baby Angel spotted the carnage, spat the dummy out and screamed even louder.

"And you knew about this too?" she asked me.

"**NO!**" I said. "Um, I've just seen this dog in the park."

That's when Dad said that his mate who works at the vet told him a story about a dog who'd come in with a suspected poisoning situation and had ended up having a life-saving operation.

"What about his owners?" I asked.

"Yes," said Mum. "What about his owners?"

That's when Dad said, "It's a bit of a **SAD STORY**."

Then he called Terrance, and Terrance bounded over and sat on Dad's lap.

Dad said that Terrance's owner didn't have enough money to pay for Terrance's follow-up medicine after his operation so they decided to give him up for adoption.

Mum's face went red. She closed her eyes and took the deepest breath I have ever seen a human take. Then she stared at Dad.

"Patrick. **WE** don't have enough money to pay for the dog's medication either."

"I know! I know!" he said. "That's why we're just **FOSTERING** him, until he's adopted. And I've got that second job now, so..."

Mum closed her eyes again and put both her hands on her head.

She did not look happy.

So that's when I said I was off to do my homework and snuck off to my room.

I watched from my bedroom window until I could see Bilal's mum getting on the bus. I rushed to the front door and shouted that I was going to Bilal's to watch a film.

No one answered.

I paused. It was **TOO** quiet.

What if Mum had killed Dad?

And the dog?

I mean, she had been spending a lot of time listening to crime podcasts.

I peeked into the living room.

EMPTY.

Then I heard a noise coming from the **CUPBOARD** in the hallway and suddenly the door opened and Mum's head poked out.

Mum was sitting on a chair, leaning back with a pen behind her ear.

"What are you doing in there?" I asked.

"Writing," she said. "This is my new **WRITING ROOM**. Every writer needs a private writing nook. I've decided this writing is no longer a hobby. I've always wanted to publish a book and this is going to be it. I just need to do a bit more research."

I could hear a true-crime podcast in the background.

That didn't really make sense to me, because that's where we kept the baked beans.

"Oh," I said.

"Have fun at Bilal's."

Then before I could say anything she disappeared back inside the cupboard and shut the door.

I had no idea where Dad, Baby Angel or the dog were. I could only hope they were alive and well.

But I didn't really have enough time to worry about that. Because I had a **PIZZA EMPIRE** to run!

Bilal answered the door.

"I have good news," he said. "We have **PRE-ORDERS**!"

I gasped.

We had pre-orders!

Bilal grinned.

"I told them we didn't open till six, but two customers put in orders anyway!"

It turns out that our illegal colour printing had **PAID OFF**. On the way home, Bilal and I had posted them through every door we passed.

And now we had actual orders! Well, only two apparently, but still!

This was **AMAZING**.

The only slight problem was that we didn't actually have any pizza yet.

"Are we going to make the pizzas ourselves?" Bilal asked. "I saw an Italian YouTube about how to make your own dough using yeast, but it takes a long time."

"Yeah, I don't think I have the skills and we definitely don't have the time. Let's buy the pizza but cut the crusts off, add some extra cheese and cook them really well."

"Sounds like a plan," Bilal agreed. "Cheapo Pizza calls for cheapo supermarket pizza!" Bilal led me to the kitchen and pointed at the stack of coins on the counter.

"I'm ready and willing to invest all that," he said.

He had **£38** in **£1** coins.

I asked Bilal why he had so many coins rather than notes.

"I like to feel the weight of my money in my pockets," said Bilal. "Any time I get some cash, I take it to the bank and ask them to change it into pound coins."

"Well, you'd better get used to notes," I said. "Because soon we're going to have enough **£1 COINS** to fill both our flats!"

Bilal grinned again. Then he pointed at me and said, "How much do you have?"

This was awkward.

I mean, this was **MY** business idea and I wanted to be the one in charge.

But I only had a tenner.

"Maybe we should each invest **£10 ONLY** to start with," I said.

"Good business move!" said Bilal. "We shouldn't invest everything all at once."

I nodded (but I didn't tell him that the **£10** Aunty Gemma had given me for Easter **WAS** everything I had!).

It didn't matter anyway.

Cheapo Pizza was going to make us **BILLIONAIRES**.

I just knew it!

My bike had a flat tyre. Luckily, Bilal's brother Yusef agreed to drive us around all night if we gave him petrol money. He was feeling generous.

Bilal said that we'd be able to pay Yusef **£10** for the night from the profit we made. He dropped us at the supermarket, then turned up the radio and said he'd wait for us in the car.

We only had half an hour to buy the pizzas and cook them before our 6 p.m. opening time on the leaflets. We rushed inside and found a huge block of cheese for **£3**. So we grabbed that and walked up and down the aisles until we found the pizzas. Then we scanned the shelves for the cheapest one. At last, Bilal said, "There!" He pointed to a huge plain cheese pizza.

The label said:

CHEESE AND TOMATO SUPREME £4

Bilal took out his phone and started calculating.

Then I remembered something the Tank had said:

It's not what you know ... it's WHO you know.

And I knew a guy who worked here.

Well, sort of.

His name was Mitch. He lived in the block next to ours and went to secondary school.

And I didn't exactly know him, but one time in the green behind our block I kicked his ball back to him and he said, "Thanks," so it wasn't like we **DIDN'T** know each other.

I told Bilal I'd be back in a minute and headed off to find Mitch.

I found him stacking a shelf.

"Hi, it's me," I said.

Mitch stared at me.

"It's Ben," I said. "The guy who kicked your ball back to you that time out on the back green."

Mitch obviously didn't remember me.

So I explained about the ball and me kicking it back to him and him being grateful.

Mitch shrugged and started stacking the shelf again.

So that's when I said that I needed a pizza.

A LOT of pizza.

I asked him what the best deal he could do was if I was willing to buy in bulk.

That's when Mitch pointed to the freezers and said, "Why don't you just buy frozen pizza? They're only **99P**."

I gasped.

I grabbed Mitch's hand and shook it hard (but not too hard this time!).

And what a deal to have made! We were going to be **RICH**!

When we got back to Bilal's house with our frozen pizza, we hit our first problem.

Storage space.

Bilal's mum's freezer was full.

We could only squeeze three pizzas in there (which meant we had seventeen left to store).

I looked at Bilal.

This was a **SERIOUS PROBLEM**.

"Maybe we should have only bought five or six pizzas," said Bilal. "I mean, we've only got two pre-orders."

So that's when I reminded Bilal what the Tank said:

GO BIG OR GO HOME TO YOUR TINY HOUSE INSTEAD OF A MANSION FULL OF CARS AND GOLD!

Bilal took a deep breath and nodded.

"You're right. Let's DO THIS."

The oven clock in Bilal's kitchen read **18:00**. It was opening time! Suddenly Bilal's mobile phone rang.

We both gasped.

It was another order!

I grabbed the phone out of Bilal's hand and answered it: "**CHEAPO PIZZA!** Best prices in town. How can we feed you?"

I had no idea what was coming out of my mouth, but it sounded amazing.

"What pizzas do you do? It doesn't say on the leaflet."

I looked at the stack of pizzas.

We'd only bought cheese. Luckily the two orders we already had were for Margherita.

"We do the best cheese pizza in town!" I replied.

Because the Tank always says to **TURN A NEGATIVE INTO A POSITIVE**.

"Is that it?" she said.

I quickly opened Bilal's fridge and looked inside.

"Um ... we do a delicious veggie pizza and, um ... a spicy chicken."

Bilal stared at me.

"I'll take one spicy chicken," said the lady.

"They're only **£4** each," I said. "Can I interest you in two delicious crust-free pizzas this evening? Our pizzas really are the best!"

"OK, I'll take a plain cheese too," she said.

It worked.

The lady gave me her address.

"Thank you for choosing Cheapo Pizza," I said. "Your order will be with you in less than ten minutes or your money back!"

Then I hung up. I was sweating.

Bilal stared at me.

"Ten minutes? Why did you say that?!"

I didn't know! It'd just come out my mouth!

"We can't use the chicken," said Bilal. "It's Mum's tea for when she gets back."

"We don't have a choice!" I said. "The customer just ordered **TWO**."

"Well, don't use it all!" said Bilal.

He was starting to panic.

"How long does it take to cook a pizza?" he asked.

That's when I realized I'd never cooked a pizza in my life! My mum always did it.

I grabbed a pizza box and read the instructions out loud: "Cooks in twelve minutes from frozen."

I gulped.

"Wait!" yelled Bilal. "They're not really frozen any more – look!"

I watched as Bilal pulled a floppy cheese pizza, which still had a bit of ice stuck on it, out of its wrapper.

"OK, go!" I said to Bilal.

Bilal looked at the floppy pizza and then back at me.

That's when I had an idea.

"We don't need an oven! We can

use the **MICROWAVE**!"

I'd used a microwave at least twice before and, from what I could remember, it was quick and easy.

I quickly cut the crusts off and Bilal grated some extra cheese on to the pizza.

I watched as Bilal tried to squeeze the pizza into the microwave.

It wouldn't fit.

"WAIT!" I yelled.

It was time to call on the wisdom of THE TANK.

THERE IS NO PROBLEM THAT'S BETTER THAN YOU ARE. YOU JUST GOTTA ATTACK PROBLEMS WITH ALL YOU GOT!

I stared at the floppy pizza.

That was it!

"Fold it in half!" I said. "We can unfold it once it's cooked!"

Bilal nodded and folded the pizza in half.

We were back on track.

With the help of the Tank, I was coming up with **IDEAS**

and **SOLVING** business problems all over the place!

Take that, Mrs Knot!

My next school report would probably say:

PROBLEM-SOLVING: COMPLETE EXCELLENCE!

It didn't take long for the first pizza to cook, then we put the spicy chicken pizza in the microwave.

By the time it was finished, we still had **SEVEN MINUTES** left to deliver it.

"Wait. How are we going to keep them flat?" said Bilal.

We hadn't thought about that!

I closed my eyes. What would the Tank do?

I had it!

"We'll use the boxes they came in. We can turn them **INSIDE OUT**!"

Bilal looked at me like he didn't understand.

So I took one of the boxes, opened it flat and then put it back together inside out.

"*Voilà*!" I said. "A plain brown pizza box! We just need a flap bit."

Bilal nodded and got scissors and cut the top of the box so it had a flap and we slid the pizza inside.

We'd done it!

Bilal wrapped the box in tin foil to keep the pizza warm.

It was time to deliver our pizza.

That's when Bilal's phone rang again. It was **ANOTHER** order!

Bilal handed the phone to me.

"**CHEAPO PIZZA!** Our pizzas are as cheap as chips! How many would you like?"

I honestly had no idea how I kept coming up with everything so fast. And it was all so good.

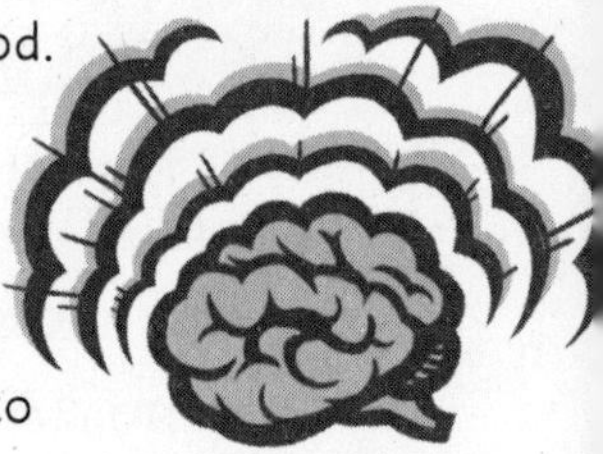

Maybe getting up at 5 a.m. really did make your brain better.

I was on a roll.

However, I could feel my hands start to sweat as the guy on the other end of the phone asked me about the pizzas.

He wanted something called "Pepperoni Passion".

We didn't have that. And I knew Bilal wouldn't let me use any more of his mum's chicken. So I told him we did a **FANTASTIC CHEESE SUPREME** and that it was the best cheese in town.

"What makes it the best?" the guy asked.

"Um ... it's a blend of white and orange Scottish cheddar melted to perfection. And it's only **£4**," I said.

He ordered **THREE**.

I couldn't believe it!

I took his address and hung up. Then I said to Bilal, "Thank goodness we've got a microwave because he wants three!"

Bilal gasped.

A car horn beeped outside. That was Yusef.

Bilal handed me a couple of pizza boxes and said, "**GO**. I'll stay here and cook." I nodded and grabbed the phone-lady's address and ran downstairs and into Yusef's car.

"What's that?" asked Yusef, peering over the top of his shades at the inside-out pizza boxes in my hand.

"**PIZZAS**," I said.

"No cooked food allowed in the Y-Man vehicle," he said. "Get rid of it."

"I'm about to get rid of them," I said. "You're taking me to **DELIVER** them."

Yusef looked at me like he had no idea what I was talking about.

That's when I realized that Bilal hadn't actually told Yusef what we were up to.

"No way!" said Yusef. "This ride needs to smell nice for the ladies. **NO FOOD ALLOWED.**"

I looked at my watch. I only had **THREE MINUTES** to deliver the pizzas.

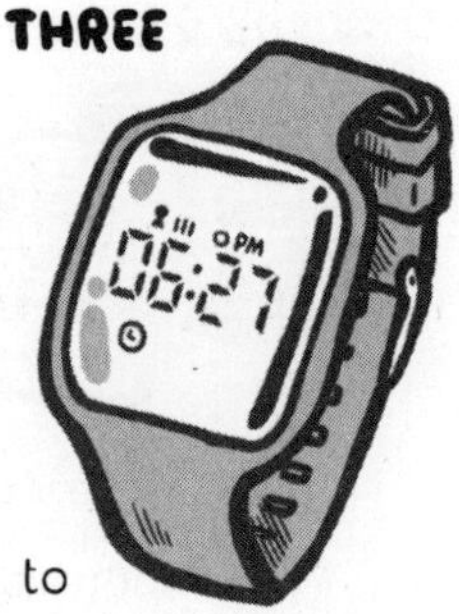

"We'll give you **£15** for the night," I said. "And I'll sit in the back and keep the windows open."

Yusef revved his engine. "Deal."

Thankfully it only took **ONE MINUTE** to get to the phone-lady's address.

I knocked.

An angry-looking lady with a baby strapped to her front opened the door.

"Here you go, miss!" I said cheerfully. "Delivered with two minutes to spare!"

The lady looked at the boxes. And then at me.

"How old are you?" she asked.

Thankfully the baby started to cry, so she took the pizzas and handed me a **£10** note and said, "Keep the change."

Then she shut the door.

A TIP.

A £2 TIP.

We hadn't even included tips in our business plan!

We were going to make even **MORE** money than I'd realized!

Yusef took me back to pick up the second order.

We delivered the three pizzas and then headed back.

But when we got back from our next delivery, things had changed.

Bilal was **FREAKING** out, the kitchen was a **MESS** and there were pizzas **EVERYWHERE**.

"The phone's been ringing non-stop!" he said. "Everyone wants a pizza!"

I smiled.

It was **WORKING**. We were giving the people what they wanted. Cheap pizza!

Yusef agreed to drop off more pizzas while we cooked them. I think he realized that he could probably get a new car for himself if he joined in on the venture. He went out with five more pizzas.

I looked around the kitchen. We were going to need a **BIGGER** headquarters (and soon). We'd probably need at least ten microwaves and at least three people working for us.

The phone rang again.

Bilal answered it and then passed it to me.

"It's for you," he whispered. "They're asking for the manager."

I loved everything about what Bilal had just said.

I was the **MANAGER**.

Soon I would be the **MANAGING DIRECTOR** of multiple Cheapo Pizza restaurants across the country. And then the world.

Pizza Hut and Domino's would go bust, obviously.

But that's just business.

I took the phone and put on my most professional voice and said, "You're speaking with the manager of the company. How may I help you?"

It was the first customer and she did **NOT** seem happy.

Something about her pizza being completely stuck to the box and having to use a knife to get it out.

She wanted a new pizza. **NOW**.

I gulped and said we'd be there in five minutes.

I grabbed the nearest pizza.

But then the phone rang again.

It was another **COMPLAINT**.

This time they said the pizza was **STUCK** and **BURNED** and **DISGUSTING**.

I looked at Bilal. He shrugged and said he might have burned one by mistake.

I opened the boxes that were waiting to go out.

Most of the pizzas were completely **STUCK** to the box. And the ones that weren't stuck to the box had **BLACK BITS** all over them.

I pointed at the black bits, but Bilal just said sorry and that he had literally **NEVER** cooked anything in his life before.

I wish he'd told me that before we'd started.

That's when things started getting **OUT OF CONTROL**.

Everyone was complaining.

They wanted **NEW** pizzas. And **REFUNDS**. Maybe it was all because of the crusts... Maybe we shouldn't have taken those off after all...

That's when Yussef poked his head into the kitchen.

"Mum's back early. You're on your own. Say one word about me and you're dead meat."

"Hello, sweethearts!" called Bilal's mum from the hall.

Yusef's head disappeared.

Bilal and I braced ourselves for impact.

The kitchen was a disaster zone.

Bilal's mum stopped in the kitchen doorway.

She gasped.

"What's **HAPPENED** to my kitchen! Did you do this, Bilal?"

Sometimes Bilal surprises me.

And sometimes he outright shocks me.

"It was **YUSEF**, Mum!" he said. "It wasn't me! I don't even know how to cook pizza, do I?"

I stared at Bilal.

He was a dead man walking (or standing).

"Yusef! Get in here now!"

Yusef appeared and did a dramatic gasp – like he had no idea what we had been doing in the kitchen.

"Bilal said you did this!" his mum cried.

Yusef stared at Bilal with his mouth wide open.

That's when Bilal mouthed at him, "You owe me."

Then he jerked his head in the direction of their bedroom and drew a big TV in the air with his fingers.

Yusef narrowed his eyes at Bilal.

"I'm sorry, Mum – it's **MY FAULT**. Bilal's right. I was just trying to show them how to cook. But the pizzas didn't turn out well. In fact, they're **TERRIBLE**."

Yusef shot us a dirty look.

That was fair enough.

"You can't even cook?" yelled Bilal's mum. "Oh, this is all my fault. I should have taught you boys how to be independent cooks before now!"

She took off her jacket and rolled up her sleeves.

"Let's start with the basics, shall we? A clean kitchen is what you need before you do anything. So let's get going. Come on! Come on! **CLEAN UP THIS MESS**, everyone!"

Bilal's mum made us clean the kitchen for almost two hours.

Bilal had put his phone on silent, but when his mum went off to watch TV we looked at it:

271 missed calls
38 voicemail messages

There was only one thing for it. We would have to go into hiding. The first step was to dispose of the phone.

Bilal offered to do Yusef's chores for a week in exchange for him driving us to the edge of town.

When we got there, we threw the phone into the river – **DRAMATICALLY**, like we were in an action film.

Then Bilal realized he didn't have a phone any more.

When I got home, I asked Mum to dye my hair...

I wasn't sure if she was going to go for it or not, but she got really excited and pulled out loads of bottles before settling on one called "Chocolate Brunette".

I looked in the mirror when Mum was finished.

I had suddenly gone from strawberry blond to chocolate brunette in thirty minutes, in three nourishing steps. I checked the packet and it wouldn't last long. But for now I looked completely different.

Now I could go into **HIDING** properly.

SATURDAY
STEP FOUR: EXPAND YOUR BUSINESS

I got up at 5 a.m., obvs.

I had a lot of **THINKING** to do after last night's disaster. The Tank always says the best thinking happens at 5 a.m.

I found Dad sleeping on the couch.

I looked around for Terrance. I couldn't see him anywhere, so I assumed Dad must have taken him to the rescue shelter. I was sad because I really felt connected to Terrance.

But then I heard snoring.

NEW snoring.

It was coming from Mum and Dad's room. I peeked inside and that's when I saw the giant dog lying on **DAD'S SIDE** of the bed, with Mum's arm draped over him.

Later, when Mum was awake and in the kitchen, I watched her feed Terrance with a spoon.

"I guess we're keeping him, then," I said.

Mum looked at Dad.

He kept his eyes on his newspaper. He was pretending not to be listening.

"Yes," she said. "I suppose Terry will have to stay."

Terry! She'd given him a **NICKNAME** already!

Dad smiled and winked at me.

I had a quick second breakfast and then got back to working on my **NEW IDEA**.

My idea was ... still **PIZZA**. With crusts back on.

People loved pizza. They'd ordered loads of it. We hadn't managed to deliver, but that didn't mean it wasn't a good idea. No, I wasn't finished with the pizza business yet.

We had **ZERO POUNDS** left. (Actually, we had zero minus the **£15** we still owed Yusef for petrol, which technically meant the business was in **DEBT**.)

But like the Tank says...

Failure only makes you want to succeed more.

And he was right.

I wanted to become a billionaire more than ever.

After breakfast, Bilal came over to my flat to have a **CRISIS MEETING**.

When I opened the door to let him in, he was wearing huge sunglasses.

"They're Yusef's," he said. "Don't tell him."

I had no intention of telling Yusef. In fact, I wanted to avoid Yusef because we still **OWED** him **£15**.

"Nice hair," said Bilal.

And then he handed me a pair of shades.

"Wear these at all times when we're out in the neighbourhood. We need to **LIE LOW** until people forget about the pizza."

I nodded and took the glasses.

Dad was at work. He'd managed to get a part-time job at Starbucks on a Saturday and a Sunday to try to earn back some of our Fake-Mongoose-Farm money.

Mum was in the cupboard, writing her book (Terry was squashed in there with her), and Baby Angel was fast asleep in her cot in Mum and Dad's room. I was in charge of keeping an eye on her, so Bilal and I held our crisis meeting there.

Bilal took his shoes off and lay down on Mum and Dad's bed.

Other people might think that that's a strange thing to do when you come to a friend's house.

But not Bilal. He's been coming over to my house since we were babies. His mum works nights sometimes, so before Yusef was old enough to look after Bilal, Bilal would stay over at mine while his mum was at work. He's basically part of the **FAMILY**. He's even called my mum "Mum" a few times by mistake!

So anyway, that's when I reminded Bilal what the Tank says about failure:

FACE YOUR FAILURES HEAD ON! WORK YOUR BUTT OFF TO FIGURE OUT WHAT CAUSED THEM AND DON'T LET THEM HAPPEN AGAIN. COMPRENDE?

"I think I've **IDENTIFIED** the number-one reason why Cheapo Pizza failed as a business. And it's not the crusts thing..." I said.

Bilal lowered his shades and looked at me. "Because we'd never cooked a pizza before?"

I shook my head.

"Because we used a microwave instead of the oven?"

I shook my head again.

"Because the pizzas were burned and stuck to the box?"

I shook my head.

It had taken me a while to figure out what our problem was too!

I'd got up at 5 a.m. and sat down at the kitchen table – **EXACTLY** like I had when I'd come up with the idea for Cheapo Pizza.

I even made sure I ate the same cereal at the same time.

And it worked.

I'd realized what our problem was!

"The pizzas were **TOO BIG**," I said. "If the pizzas had been smaller, we wouldn't have had to fold them to fit them in the microwave."

Bilal gasped. "And the cheese wouldn't have gone all weird, sticky and stringy and stuck to the box."

Bilal stared at me with eager eyes.

"So what now? We buy smaller pizzas?" he asked.

I shook my head.

Because the Tank says:

If something ain't working, maybe it's time to do a total ONE-EIGHTY and come up with a totally different and WILD idea! People might not get you at first, but that's all right. Sometimes it takes people a while to appreciate GREATNESS.

I smiled at Bilal.

"Wrong. We're going to buy **BIGGER** pizzas!" I said.

Bilal looked confused.

"We'll buy the biggest, cheapest pizzas we can find and sell pizza by the **SLICE** and make a huge **PROFIT**!" I told him.

"But we don't have any money left," Bilal said. "How are we going to buy pizza?"

He had a point.

"Well, yes, but we've got this to help us figure it out."

I picked up the Tank's book and held it up.

We read in complete silence for a while until we came across a bit that said:

No one gets to the top alone. Even BILLIONAIRES need help. If you're reading this and thinking "I NEED HELP" then, my friend, it's high time to get yourself a MENTOR. Someone who's totally SMASHING IT in the business world. Go and ask them for some advice ... NOW!

Abra-Kebabra was the most popular kebab shop on our street.

"Let me do the talking," I said as I opened the door.

Bilal nodded, then he put his shades on and nudged me to do the same.

"One of our pizza customers might be inside," he said.

I nodded and put on the shades, and we stepped into the shop.

It smelled **DELICIOUS**.

I was aware that we looked a bit young, so I put on my deepest voice and asked to speak to the manager. I was hoping the shades would help.

The guy behind the counter didn't say anything. He just stared at me.

Then a huge guy shaving a massive leg of kebab looked over his shoulder at us and said, "I'm the manager. You have a problem?"

"Yes," I said, in my deep voice. "We do have a problem and we're hoping you might be able to help us."

The man put down his shaver and turned to face us.

"You want free chips, right? We don't do that."

I looked at Bilal, and we both shook our heads.

"No thank you," I said politely, although the chips smelled delicious.

"What we really want is some advice."

The guy looked us up and down for a moment and then he said, "OK. Ask me."

I took a deep breath.

This was it. This was what the Tank called an "in".

An important **OPPORTUNITY.**

I wasn't going to waste it.

This was a business owner. The owner of the most

popular kebab shop in town. And I had him here, right now, listening to me. Willing to give us advice about our business and becoming billionaires.

I explained that we had started a revolutionary pizza takeaway business the night before called Cheapo Pizza and that we'd had loads of orders, but we had made a mistake and now we had a cash-flow problem and needed a mentor to guide us and give us advice on the next stage of our inspirational journey, so we could become the best pizza takeaway in town!

I used words like **INSPIRATIONAL** and **JOURNEY** because the Tank says that when you have a **VISION** you need to be **PASSIONATE** when speaking to other people about it so they **BELIEVE IN YOU**.

When I'd finished, Bilal put his fist out to the side and I gave it a pump.

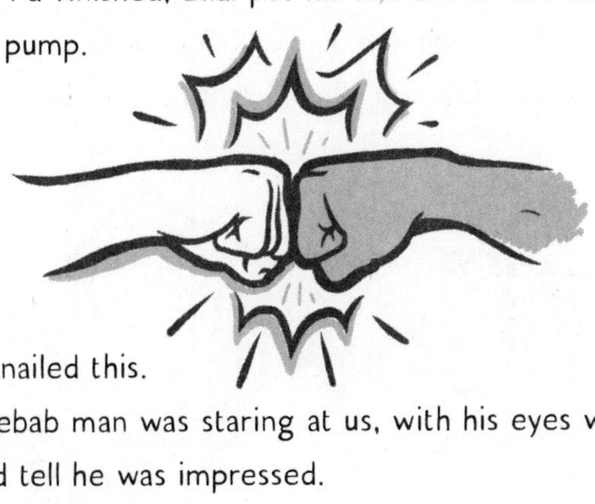

We'd nailed this.

The kebab man was staring at us, with his eyes wide.

I could tell he was impressed.

Then suddenly he slammed both his huge hands down on the counter, and Bilal and I both jumped.

"You!" he bellowed at us. "You are the reason for no pizza orders last night! You are **THIS**?"

He reached under the counter and pulled out one of our coloured leaflets.

"You are trying to put me out of business, yes?"

That's when I noticed the giant neon pizza sign above the man's head. They sold pizzas too.

"You want advice, little men?" he said.

We watched, frozen to the spot, as the giant kebab man rubbed his huge hands together.

"You **FORGET** about this Cheapo Pizza and maybe you **LIVE** another day!"

We both nodded and ran out of Abra-Kebabra as fast as we could and hid in the alley next to Starbucks.

I was watching TV with Dad in the living room this morning when Mum ran into the room and peeked through the blinds.

Then she **GASPED** and pulled the curtains shut.

"Get down!" she hissed, dropping to her knees and scrambling across the living-room carpet.

Dad asked if it was Gran. I remembered that one time when Gran had tried to come for a surprise – Mum had made us hide behind the sofa while Gran rang the doorbell over and over.

"It's the **LANDLORD**," said Mum.

Dad's face fell.

"We can't let him in in case he sees the dog!" added Mum. "I don't think we're allowed pets!"

Dad dropped to his knees and pulled me off the sofa with him.

"Where's the dog?" he asked, panicked.

"Asleep in the hall! But he'll wake up if that doorbell goes!"

Dad scuttled across the living room and out into the hall, where he tried to pull Terry out of the basket.

"He's really heavy! He won't wake up!" said Dad.

Mum scuttled forward and grabbed Terry by the back legs and started to pull him (and the basket) along the hallway's laminate flooring.

Terry **STILL** didn't wake up.

Mum got sleeping Terry halfway down the hall when a **SHADOW** appeared behind the glass at the front door.

Everyone froze.

Terry started to **SNORE**. Even louder than Angel.

I held my breath and waited for the doorbell to ring.

Terry was going to go nuts.

I had to do something.

I remembered something the Tank had said:

Find out what people REALLY want. And then give it to them.

Terry loved barking at the doorbell.

But he loved **SLIPPERS** more.

The shadow raised its arm to ring the doorbell.

So I slid along the hallway floor, pulling Mum's slipper off her foot as I passed her, and **SHOVED** it in front of Terry's mouth just as the doorbell **RANG** and Terry's eyes burst **OPEN**.

We all stared at Terry.

His eyes sort of rolled around, like there was too much excitement going on.

He looked at the door.

Then down at the slipper in front of his mouth.

That's when he started munching Minnie Mouse's head off.

We all let out a (very quiet) sigh of relief.

We waited for the landlord to ring the doorbell again. But he didn't. He just posted something through the letterbox and left.

Once we were sure he was gone, Mum scuttled forward and picked up the letter and opened it.

She started crying.

She handed the letter to Dad.

He looked a bit like he might start crying too!

I crawled over and looked at the words in **BOLD** across of the top of the page.

This was bad.

Really **BAD**.

Because at the top of the letter the words said:

FINAL NOTICE - 15 DAYS' NOTICE OF EVICTION

We were getting kicked out of our flat.

Mum was staring at Dad.

"Final notice? **FINAL?**" she shouted.

Dad was lying still on his stomach. Playing dead.

"Patrick!"

Dad slowly turned and rolled over on to his back.

"I'm sorry," he said. "I've been trying to fix it so you wouldn't even have to know."

"Well, I **KNOW** now!" screamed Mum.

"I've had to take a bit of a pay cut at work because the business has been struggling – but it's only temporary! It means that I haven't exactly been able to pay the rent in full for the past couple of months. It's getting sorted, though, and I'll be able to pay the rent soon. Don't worry. I'm on it!"

Mum looked like she was going to be sick.

"How much do we owe, Patrick?"

"It's fine, love. It'll be sorted soon!" said Dad, getting up. "Please don't worry. With my new job at Starbucks, I'll be able to pay the bill at the end of the month and no one will be getting evicted. Don't even think about it again! I promise!"

I couldn't help but spot that Dad had his fingers crossed behind his back.

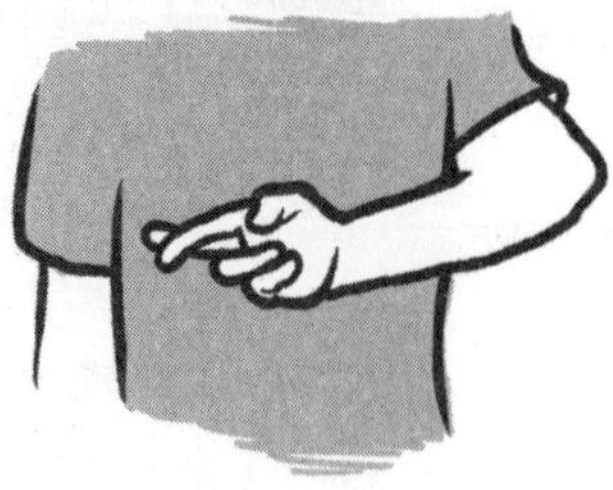

We were in **TROUBLE**.

Mum started shouting about how we could have used our **SAVINGS** if he hadn't bought the non-existent **MONGOOSE FARM**.

Then she threw the notice on the floor and stormed off. Dad gave me a quick "I'm sorry" look and ran after her.

I picked up the notice and read it.

We owed **£1,000**.

That was a lot of money.

And we only had fifteen days to pay it.

Or we'd be **EVICTED**.

I wandered through to the living room.

Dad had his arm around Mum.

"Where are we going to go if we can't get the money in time?" said Mum between sobs.

Baby Angel was crying now too, because Terry was eating Minnie Mouse's insides (which must have been pretty terrifying for a two-year-old to witness).

"That won't happen! Work will pay me before then, I promise!" said Dad.

"But what if it DOES happen, Patrick?" said Mum.

"It won't but if it DID then I suppose we'd have to go to my mum's," said Dad.

Mum stopped sobbing immediately.

"**OVER YOUR DEAD BODY!**" she said.

With the amount of crime writing Mum was doing, I was beginning to worry that **THAT** might actually be the case!

Dad left for work. A few minutes later, Bilal came round. We needed to have a serious meeting about the **FUTURE** of our business.

But I didn't want to tell him about the eviction.

He was dreaming of **PENTHOUSE APARTMENTS** and **SPORTS CARS** and had mentioned something about a deluxe **ICE-CREAM MACHINE**.

I didn't want to put a downer on things by telling him I might need to use the money for rent if Dad's pay problem didn't get sorted in time.

I think Dad had managed to convince Mum that it would get sorted in time to pay the huge rent bill.

But I couldn't stop thinking about Dad crossing his fingers behind his back when he promised it would all be fine.

"I think we should stay inside today," said Bilal, shutting my bedroom curtains. "I don't want to risk bumping into Abra-Kebabra Man. I had a nightmare last night that he wrapped me up in donor meat and rolled me down a big hill into a field of cows. It was terrifying!"

"I don't think you need to worry about that," I said. "I mean, even if that DID happen, and it won't, cows don't eat donor kebab."

Bilal looked at me, stunned.

"These ones did!" he yelled.

"I think we should go out for a walk," I said. The Tank always says you make better decisions after some exercise. "We could go and see Dad in Starbucks and he could make us some free hot chocolates."

"OK," said Bilal. "I'll meet you outside. I need to get something first."

When Bilal eventually appeared outside, I barely recognized him.

He was wearing one of his mum's long coats and a massive woolly hat. And the shades.

He couldn't have stood out more if he'd tried.

Unfortunately, there was only **ONE WAY** to get to Starbucks and that meant we had to pass Abra-Kebabra.

It had to be done. Besides, we were going to have to walk past it at some point because our school was at the end of the street. We may as well get it over with.

We sped up as we got closer.

"Keep your eyes forward!" said Bilal.

I nodded but couldn't help looking inside.

I stopped.

"Why are you **STOPPING**?" Bilal hissed.

"Look," I said. "It's closed. They don't open until five o'clock."

Bilal relaxed and let out a deep breath.

But then suddenly someone banged on the window from inside. We gasped. Kebab Man was inside, shaking his giant fist at us!

We **RAN** all the way to Starbucks. I basically had to carry Bilal inside, because he was even more unfit than I was and also because he'd tripped on his mum's long coat and twisted his ankle.

I dumped Bilal on a comfy sofa at the back and went to get our hot chocolates.

Dad hadn't spotted us yet. He was behind the counter looking a bit stressed while a lady shouted, "Skinny on the side. On the side!"

It obviously wasn't the right time to ask for free hot chocolates, so I just poured two waters from the help-yourself jug and sat down on the sofa with Bilal.

Bilal refused to take his hat and shades off (even though Kebab Man had already recognized him).

"You OK?" I asked.

Bilal nodded that he was.

But then he drank all his water in one go and then he drank mine too.

"You know he's just trying to scare us off because we're the competition?" I said.

"Well, it's working!" said Bilal. "Did you see the size of his hands?"

I nodded.

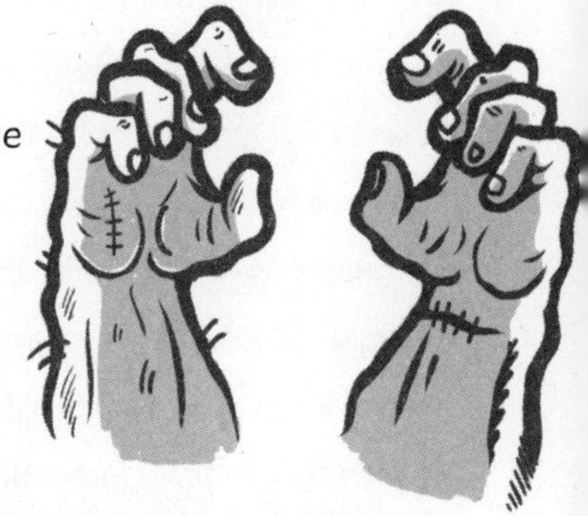

It was impossible not to see the size of them.

They were monstrous.

It was time to change the subject. I didn't want Bilal giving himself more nightmares.

"Let's get back to planning our new business," I said. The Tank says that sometimes all you need is to rebrand. "Cheapo Pizza is officially dead. We're now **CHEAPO SLICE O'PIZZA**."

I put my hand in my pocket and pulled out Mum's old pay-as-you-go phone I'd found in the kitchen drawer.

"And we have a new business phone!" I said. "With a new phone number."

Bilal stared at the ancient phone.

"New name, new concept, new phone," I said. "We're starting afresh."

Even if there wasn't a huge, kebab-shaving man to worry about, I still would've changed the name of the business after all the complaints we got on opening night.

That's what my Uncle Donnie did when he fell through a window and landed on a wedding cake, flattening it and splattering it all over the bride's dress. He changed the name of his window-cleaning business from The Window King to The Professional and Reliable Window Company – so that his new customers wouldn't realize it was him.

"I'm still worried about the kebab man," Bilal said. "He'll find out we're selling pizzas whatever we're called."

I smiled.

I'd had an **IDEA**.

A brilliant idea.

It had **PINGED** into my head when I saw the "closed" sign on the window at Abra-Kebabra.

"Abra-Kebabra opens at five o'clock," I said. "So we're going to operate during the **DAYTIME** when Abra-Kebabra is closed."

Bilal shook his head, like he was trying to get his brain to work. "But we'll be at **SCHOOL** during the day."

I smiled and put my hand on Bilal's shoulder.

"**EXACTLY!**" I said.

MONDAY

FOURTEEN DAYS UNTIL EVICTION

It didn't take long to explain my **VISION** to Bilal.

"Picture our school dinners," I told him.

He made a face.

"Exactly!" I said.

I mean, some of the stuff the dinner ladies served us was OK (the macaroni and cheese was actually quite good!) but a lot of it was **BAD**.

And that had given me an idea.

I reminded Bilal of something the Tank says:

If people aren't satisfied with what's on offer, then give them a BETTER OPTION and you'll make a lot of money!

"So what if we gave everyone at school another option?"

Bilal stared at me.

"What if we moved our pizza business into the playground and let people buy a **SLICE OF PIZZA** for their lunch instead? We'd have to keep it a **SECRET**, of course," I added. "I'm pretty sure Mr Ferrier would not be happy about us setting up a pizza restaurant in the playground ... and the dinner ladies might kill us if they found out!"

Bilal's mouth dropped open.

He kept staring.

So I kept going.

"We can spread the word throughout the day, then serve the pizza from the far end of the playground next to the big bush. The teachers never go down there!"

I'd thought of everything.

Bilal started to speak.

I knew what he was going to say. He was going to say I was amazing.

"But we don't have any money left to buy pizzas," he said.

OK. So he hadn't actually said that I was amazing (but he was obviously thinking it).

I smiled. This was the truly **GENIUS** part. It was like the Tank said. Sometimes you have to take risks to make cash.

"Not a problem. We're going to get a **BANK LOAN**!"

After school, back at my flat, Bilal took out a black leather folder and showed me what he'd been working on when he was meant to be doing maths.

It was a **BUSINESS PLAN**.

I asked Bilal where he got the fancy folder and he just said, "School."

Bilal sometimes borrows things from school (and I'm not exactly sure if he asks permission), so I decided not to question it. That way, if the teachers find out and ask me about it, I can say, "I have absolutely no idea where Bilal got the folder." (And almost mean it.)

So, anyway, Bilal said we needed to be **PREPARED** if we were going to ask the bank for a business loan. Then he smiled and tapped his finger on the fancy folder and said, "Once they see this baby, they'll be willing to give us whatever we need!"

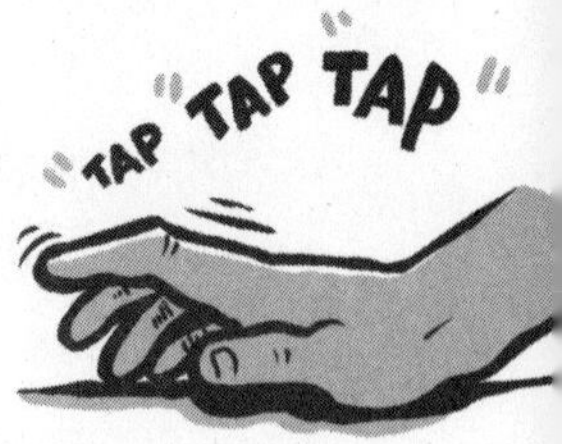

I was shocked when I looked inside.

Bilal had drawn loads of pizzas with numbers next to them and then slices of pizza with numbers inside those too, to show how much more money we could make by selling by the slice.

There were **EQUATIONS** and **GRAPHS** and **BAR CHARTS** and loads of **£ SIGNS** everywhere to show how much money we were going to make.

And the amounts got higher and higher each month! It was amazing.

I was pretty sure that if we took this to the bank it wouldn't matter that we were only ten years old.

All that would matter was that this would probably be one of the best business plans they'd ever seen.

Bilal said that, based on his calculations, the bank would be making a bad choice not to give us a loan. Then he said that he was even willing to have the bank's name written on the

side of the pizza boxes as as our sponsor if they wanted.

"If you're happy with that," he said, looking up at me. "After all, you're the manager."

In that moment, I realized that, even though we were partners, it was up to me to make the final decision about the bank loan and any sponsorship that we would be willing to accept from them. I had to take this seriously.

I told Bilal to go home and put on the **SMARTEST** clothes that he had.

I found Dad's funeral tie and put that on.

I also found my school blazer and tucked one of Mum's hair-scarf things into the blazer pocket and draped it over the school badge, so no one would know it was a school blazer. Not only did the scarf cover the school logo, it also looked really **FANCY**, like I was from London or something!

I went to look in the bathroom mirror.

My hair was a mess.

Dad didn't use anything on his hair. But Mum did.

I picked up something that said "Sleek Dry Shampoo" on it and sprayed loads on my hair and used Mum's brush to make it look tidy.

When I was finished, I checked myself in the mirror.

I didn't look bad, actually. And I definitely didn't look ten any more. There were even streaks of white running through my hair!

I shouted to Mum that I was going to Bilal's before tea and ran out of the door before anyone could see me.

When I met Bilal at the bank, I wasn't sure what to say.

He'd gone in a different direction than I had clothes-wise.

He was wearing his school shirt with no tie and what looked like his mum's shiny black trousers that she wears when she goes out to the pub with my mum.

I looked down at Bilal's feet. He was wearing giant white-and-pink trainers.

"They're Yusef's new trainers. He'll kill me if he knows I'm wearing them."

He lifted up a foot and I saw that he'd wrapped cling film around them.

"So they don't get marks on the soles," he said.

"These were the most expensive clothes I could find in the house," he added.

Maybe this was a good thing.

If we both went in wearing suits, we might look a bit boring. This way, I'd look like the **SERIOUS BUSINESSMAN** who knew I could take this business global. And Bilal would look like the **CREATIVE GUY** who would make sure our pizza restaurants were awesome and different to anything anyone had ever seen!

I smiled.

This was going to work.

THE GREAT BANK LOAN

I took a deep breath and put both hands on the glass doors of the bank and pushed them wide open.

The Tank says that when you enter a room, you should open both doors when you walk through so you can make a **PROPER ENTRANCE**.

But the doors were really heavy.

Once I'd opened both doors, I didn't really know how to let them go without them crashing back into Bilal and smashing all over the street! I just stood there, with my arms outstretched, holding both doors open while everyone inside the bank stared at me.

The Tank was right.

This was how you made an entrance and get **NOTICED**.

Bilal ducked under one of my arms and helped me shut the doors. Then we walked up to the woman behind the counter.

The woman gave us a weird look. "Um, can I help you?"

Bilal and I looked at each other.

We knew exactly what to say. We'd **PRACTISED** it all the way home from school.

I cleared my throat and used the deepest voice I could manage. "Yes. We have a very important meeting with the bank manager."

The women looked at me.

And then at Bilal.

Then she looked at Bilal's **GIANT SHOES**.

"Is he expecting you?" she said.

"Oh," I said. "He'll be very excited to see us."

I gave her my biggest smile.

The woman picked up her phone and covered her mouth as she whispered something down the line.

"Take a seat over there," she said when she was done. "The manager will be with you in a moment."

It had worked! We were **IN**!

We sat on the tiny sofa. Bilal placed the leather folder on the glass table and dusted the top of it.

I looked at his shoes.

They were **MASSIVE**.

I mean, Yusef's feet must be at least five sizes bigger than Bilal's. I wondered how Bilal was managing to keep them on his feet without them flying off when he walked.

I was about to ask him if he'd stuffed them with socks or something, when a door opened and a really tall man wearing a suit and black-rimmed glasses appeared.

"Gentlemen, I understand we have an appointment today, is that correct?"

We both leapt up.

"Yes, sir!" I said.

I picked up the leather folder and looked him RIGHT into his eyes and said, "There's something in here that you need to see."

I didn't smile.

I didn't blink.

I didn't move my face at all.

And neither did Bilal.

Just like we had planned.

This was called a **POWER MOVE** (we'd watched the Tank do it on the documentary).

The bank manager gave us a strange look, but then he stepped to the side and pointed his hand to his office and said to come in.

And at that point I really wanted to smile!

MY PLAN WAS WORKING!

I knew I had to stay in the zone, though, and keep doing the power move.

Bilal and I went into the office. The bank manager invited us to take a seat, so we did. Then he sat directly across from us at his big desk and asked us what we would like to talk to him about.

I took a deep breath and explained **CHEAPO SLICE O' PIZZA**.

Even though we had rehearsed it over and over, I was a bit worried that I might stumble. Like when I have to talk in front of the class (which I hate doing!).

But I didn't stumble at all.

Not once.

When I was finished, I looked at Bilal and saw that he had tears streaming down his face.

That was a surprise because, even though I knew how good my speech had been, I hadn't expected Bilal to be so moved by it that he'd start weeping.

But then I noticed that Bilal wasn't blinking and I realized he was still doing the power move and **THAT** that was why he had tears running down his face.

I gave Bilal the **NOD** (which is a secret signal between two business partners that lets the other one know when it's their turn to talk).

Bilal wiped his face with his sleeve and stood up.

He opened the leather folder. He took a pen out of his shirt pocket and started pointing at the **SLICES OF PIZZA** and **NUMBERS** and **GRAPHS**.

I watched in amazement as he stood there, not blinking, doing really difficult calculations out loud to the bank manager.

Then, when Bilal was finished with the numbers, he started waving his arms around, talking about how this wasn't just pizza and that it was a pizza **REVOLUTION**. And that everyone should be able to afford takeaway pizza, and that we were going to make that dream a reality and **CHANGE THE WORLD**.

At the end of his speech, he grinned at me and I winked because he was awesome.

Bilal sat back down and we both stared at the bank manager, waiting to see what he was going to say.

He smiled and took off his glasses and told us that that might have been one of the **BEST** business pitches he'd ever heard in his life!

"How old are you, boys?" he asked.

My heart started to sink.

I knew that, when it comes to business, the best thing in the world is to be **HONEST**. Because the Tank always says:

Be yourself,
be honest,
be awesome!

"We're ten," I said (using my normal voice).

The gig was up.

The bank manager nodded.

"Well," he said. "I'm not allowed to give bank loans to ten-year-olds. But what I can do is give you some **ADVICE**."

We both stared at him.

"Keep doing what you're doing," he said. "Keep coming up with ideas like this one. Keep pushing forward. Keep trying. And come back here when you're eighteen and I'll see what I can do for you. Because I've got a feeling that you guys are going to do something big, and I think that I would quite like to be a part of it."

Then he stood up, so we stood up too. I put my hand out to shake his and he smiled and shook my hand.

I made sure I shook it **FIRMLY (BUT NOT TOO FIRMLY!)** just like Bilal and I had practised.

As we were leaving, I felt weird. I mean, we didn't get the loan we'd hoped to get, but an actual bank manager had told us that he thought our idea was good and that we were going to be big.

But it didn't really help us with our new business venture.

I turned to Bilal.

He looked a bit like he was going to start crying, so I thought it was best to get him out of there while we still had our dignity.

I loosened my tie and took a big breath of fresh air as we left the bank.

I wasn't sure what we were going to do now, though.

That's when we heard fast, clicking footsteps approaching and turned to see the lady from the bank reception running after us.

I looked down to make sure that Bilal had remembered to pick up the leather folder, but Bilal had it in his hands.

"Wait!" she called. "I heard your pitch." She reached inside her bag. "You guys were great ... and I hated school dinners!"

Then she **HANDED** us a **£10** note!

"You can give me it back when you start making money. Good luck!"

With that, she smiled and walked back to the bank.

Bilal and I looked at each other.

We were in shock.

We'd done it!

It was half of what we were hoping for.

But it was still half.

We'd got a **LOAN**!

TUESDAY

THIRTEEN DAYS UNTIL EVICTION

The next day, we arrived at school with our school bags full of pizza. We'd used the **£10** bank loan to buy ten frozen pizzas for **£1** each on the way to school.

We'd had to buy smaller pizzas than we'd wanted, so that we could hide them in our school bags, but I was sure we could still make a huge **PROFIT** by selling them by the slice.

Bilal said that they would be perfectly thawed by lunchtime and ready to slice.

The plan was to cut each of the ten pizzas into six slices, which would give us sixty slices in total.

We were going to sell those slices for **£1** each, which meant that if we sold them all, we would have **£60**.

As soon as we walked into class, I regretted my plan.

Mr Ferrier, the head, was there.

He said that he would be taking our class today because Mrs Knot was ill and he was looking forward to collecting our maths homework.

I looked at Bilal and he seemed just as worried as I was.

We'd had to empty our bags to make room for all the pizzas. Which meant we'd had to leave our workbooks behind.

We knew we were going to take some heat for that.

But like the Tank said:

Sometimes you have to make HARD CHOICES to make it to the top and achieve your DREAMS.

I hadn't been looking forward to telling Mrs Knot that I didn't have my homework with me. But now we were in an even worse situation because we had to tell the actual **HEAD TEACHER** that we didn't have our homework with us!

However, getting into trouble for not doing our homework and forgetting our PE kit was **SMALL POTATOES** compared to what we might get caught doing.

Because what we had planned was this:

1. Smuggle two bags full of pizza into school.

2. Set up a secret pizza business in the playground.

3. Sneak into the staffroom before lunch and cook the pizzas using the teachers' microwave without getting caught.

We were hoping to sneak into the staffroom just before lunch and cook the slices of pizza as fast as we could.

We'd practised cooking pizza at home. We had the cooking time down to twenty seconds to heat two slices of pizza at the same time using the highest microwave setting.

Bilal had done all the calculations. He reckoned that, if we got into the staffroom before lunch, we could cook sixty slices of pizza in ten minutes.

And it was up to me to buy us those ten minutes in the staffroom.

Now, though, Bilal was having serious second thoughts about the plan, because the head teacher was going to be our teacher for the day.

Bilal handed me pieces of folded paper all morning while Mr Ferrier was looking at the computer. He'd written "**ABORT PLAN**" and "**WE'RE GOING TO GET CAUGHT**" and "**I CAN FEEL SOMETHING LEAKING OUT OF MY BAG**".

So I wrote a message back saying that we were not giving up and to **STICK TO THE PLAN**.

And also that the leaking was just the pizzas defrosting in our bags (which was the plan and why we were keeping our bags on our backs, so that our body heat would defrost them so we could cook them quicker).

Mr Ferrier asked us to open our maths workbooks. I gave Bilal the nod.

Bilal slipped off his chair and on to the floor.

Everyone stared at Bilal.

"It's OK! He's going to be OK!"

I said. "He fell off his chair and hurt his leg and needs to go and see the nurse. I'll take him."

Mr Ferrier came rushing over. He went on his school walkie-talkie and asked the nurse to come.

Bilal and I looked at each other.

This wasn't the plan.

We had planned that I would take Bilal to the nurse. That way we both got out of class. But we wouldn't actually go to the nurse. The plan was that we would go straight to the staffroom and start cooking the pizzas!

Bilal opened his mouth to say something.

But before he could say a word, the classroom door flew open and the school nurse whisked Bilal and his backpack full of defrosting pizza away.

I sat down with my own bag full of defrosting pizza on my back.

This was a problem.

A **BIG** problem.

I had to think quick.

I put up my hand and asked if I could go to the toilet.

Mr Ferrier looked at his watch. "Um, it's a bit close to lunchtime to be going to the toilet," he said.

I didn't say anything. I just stared at him.

Mr Ferrier tapped his watch and said, "Can it not wait?"

I shook my head really fast so that he would think I was bursting.

Mr Ferrier sighed and nodded.

I ran out of the class all the way to the staffroom because it was now **UP TO ME** to sneak into the staffroom and cook all the pizzas in my backpack.

And I only had **TEN MINUTES** to do it in.

When I got to the staffroom, the door was closed.

I looked at my watch.

Nine minutes left before the lunch bell went.

I checked to make sure that no one was coming and then I put my hand out and

slowly started to open the door, so I could peek inside to make sure there were no teachers in there.

That's when I heard a noise.

I gasped.

There weren't supposed to be any teachers in the staffroom!

They were all teaching!

I was about to slowly close the door and run away when I smelled something.

It was coming from the staffroom.

I recognized that delicious cheesy smell.

It was **PIZZA**.

Our **CHEAPO SLICE O' PIZZA.**

I pushed the door open a little further and peeked inside.

It was Bilal!

Bilal was mega happy to see me.

He said that he'd told the nurse he felt much better and that she'd let him go and that he'd come straight to the staffroom.

Bilal had cooked most of his pizza already by the looks of things, and he was ready for my bagload!

I quickly started putting all the cooked slices of pizza in the Tupperware boxes we'd brought with us, carefully placing a piece of greaseproof paper between each slice, just like we'd planned, so that the slices of pizza didn't stick together.

As the Tank says, **ALWAYS KEEP LEARNING**.

And we had learnt a lot since our first pizza disaster!

The final pizza came out of the microwave with one minute to spare.

There wasn't any cleaning up to do, because we'd left the pizza wrapping at home and had put the frozen pizzas directly into our bags to let them defrost.

We packed the Tupperware boxes into our backpacks and got out of the staffroom **JUST** as the bell for lunch went.

OK... The pizzas were ready but we still had to stop by the store cupboard and borrow one of the folding tables to put our slices on for selling.

I was the lookout while Bilal unlocked the store cupboard next to the boys' toilets and slipped inside.

Bilal reappeared with a small, folded table.

"Let's go!" he said, checking to make sure no one was around.

We ran across the playground to the very far end, keeping close to the side of the school building at all times, so we wouldn't be spotted from a window by a teacher. Then we set up our table right next to the big bush, so you definitely couldn't see us from the school building.

We opened the Tupperware boxes and lay the slices of warm pizza on the blue paper tissues we'd taken from the boys' toilets at break.

With that, we were done! We stood back and waited for our first customer to arrive.

It didn't take long.

Word had spread quickly at breaktime about the pop-up pizza stall near the big bush.

And it just so happened that today was **FISH FAJITA DAY** for school dinners, so we'd hit the jackpot.

Within about five minutes, we had a huge queue waiting for a helping of **CHEAPO SLICE O' PIZZA**.

I was serving the pizza, while Bilal was taking the money and doing the change, because he was much better than me at calculating how much change to give.

But then the line got so **BIG** we became worried that it was going to lead all the way back to the school building – like a trail for one of the teachers to spot and follow! So we decided to make two lines and we both served and took the money. I was much better at calculating the change than I thought I would be.

It must have been all the extra maths I was doing out of school!

"The lines are getting too big," said Bilal. "We're going to get caught."

"Maybe. Maybe not," I said. "Just keep serving."

If we were going to get shut down, it was important that we made as much money as we could before it happened.

"I think we should stop," said Bilal.

He was starting to panic and I had to calm him down.

We couldn't stop.

I wasn't sure Dad was going to be able to pay the rent.

We HAD to keep going.

That's when I saw someone running towards us.

FAST.

I'd recognize that run anywhere.

It was **APRIL MAY**.

She stopped in front of the pizza table, standing with her hands on her hips. "You're trying to make lots of money. Well, I know how you could make more. Do you want me to help?"

Me and Bilal gawked at each other.

We weren't really used to girls talking to us.

Especially April May.

She's, like, the best at everything.

April May stared at us, waiting for an answer, but we didn't really know what to say, so we didn't say anything.

"Well, let me know if you change your mind," she said. "Oh, and ... the teacher's coming. GO!"

Straight away, Bilal and I shoved the rest of the pizza into his backpack, then I collapsed the table and threw it into the big bush.

And we ran.

We hid in an empty classroom and emptied the Tupperware of money on to a desk, then carefully counted it.

We'd made **£56**.

We'd sold **FIFTY-FIVE** slices of pizza (we knew that because we only had five squashed ones left at the bottom of Bilal's bag) and one kid had given us a **£1** tip.

Bilal grabbed a pen and said he needed to do some **FINANCIAL FORECASTING** for the week.

I didn't know what that meant, but he looked really excited about it, so I handed him a pen and watched Bilal's eyes get wider and wider as he did his calculations.

Then he gasped and actually dropped the pen.

"We could have over **£200** by Friday if we keep going like this!"

We stared at each other.

And then we burst out laughing.

We couldn't believe it!

We'd done it.

We'd started a **SUCCESSFUL** business.

We were going to be **RICH**!

After maths and English, we got called to an emergency assembly.

Mr Ferrier got up on stage and said that six pupils had gone home with **SICKNESS** and most of the toilets were out of order.

Apparently there was a rumour going round that someone had been selling pizza in the playground.

I held my breath.

I wanted to turn and look at Bilal, but I didn't want to do anything that would make us look suspicious.

My brain was **WHIRRING**.

Bilal tugged on my shirt sleeve.

"The pizzas must have gone bad in our bags!" he hissed.

That wasn't possible.

We had been defrosting them!

"I have information that one small boy and one tall boy were involved," said Mr Ferrier.

We were in **BIG TROUBLE**.

Then someone a few rows in front of us shouted, "It was the secondary-school kids. They snuck through the fence at the back. I saw them. There's a hole in the fence, you know? My dad phoned you about it a few weeks ago. Has no one fixed it yet?"

Mr Ferrier looked a bit flustered.

"Um. Yes. Yes! I'm well aware of the hole in the fence! Be assured we will deal with that and with the secondary school pupils involved."

I turned and looked at Bilal.

We were **SAVED**.

As we were walking out of assembly, April May grabbed my hand in hers and I almost choked.

Then she rushed out and I felt something in my hand.

It was a scrunched-up ball of paper.

I squeezed my hand into a fist, keeping the ball of paper safe, and walked back to class with my heart thumping in my chest the whole way.

I waited until everyone was settled in their seats, then I asked to go to the toilet.

And as soon as I was alone in the corridor, I opened it.

It said:

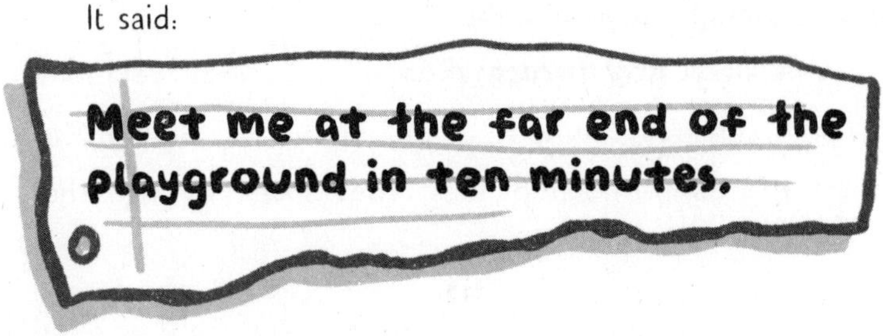

I ran all the way there.

When I got there, April May was on her hands and knees, pulling at the fence.

"Help me!" she said.

I had no idea what we were doing, but I helped her pull at the fence until the side snapped and came loose and we both fell backwards.

"There," she said. "Your cover story. A **BROKEN** fence."

I looked at the fence, then at April May's grinning face.

The fence hadn't been broken, but now it was.

She was unbelievable.

April May got up, dusted herself off, then ran back to the school building.

"Wait!" I called after her. "You want to join our pizza business?"

April May stopped. Then she nodded and said, "I'd love that."

Bilal was NOT happy with me.

"I should at least be consulted in big business decisions like this!" he said.

He was right.

"Do we even need her?" he asked. "I mean, wouldn't it be better as just us?"

I reminded Bilal about what the Tank said about there being "**STRENGTH IN NUMBERS**".

He also said: "**TEAMWORK MAKES FAST WORK**."

And I needed our business to grow faster!

Bilal wasn't convinced.

He said that a new business partner at this early stage was too risky and that April May probably only wanted to be part of our business because she'd seen our success at lunchtime and thought it was going to be all easy and glamorous and that she'd probably run off if things got tough.

I stared at Bilal and said, "Does April May seem like the kind of person who would run off if things get tough?"

Bilal looked at me for a moment and then shook his head.

Exactly.

April May was one of the **TOUGHEST** people we knew!

She was the one who'd stood up to our old teacher, Mr Hips, when he tried to give us all triple homework during the Christmas holidays. April May had contacted the local press and got on the radio and the TV about it!

Now all the teachers in our town are

banned by the council from issuing any homework over the festive family period.

"Why would she want to help us?" said Bilal.

"No idea!" I said. "But let's find out."

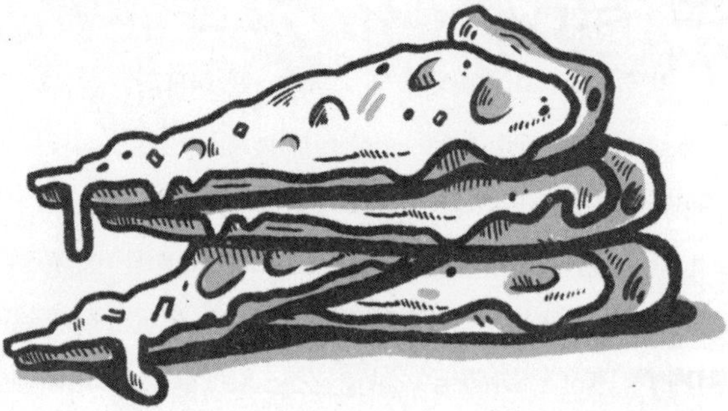

SATURDAY

NINE DAYS UNTIL EVICTION

We had to put a hold on our selling-pizza-at-school idea, but on Saturday Bilal and I met April May at the train station.

"For this pizza business to work, we need crowds," she said. "And when it's a **NICE** day like today, the beach is super **BUSY**! That's where you should sell pizza." She looked at me. "You've got the pizza, right?" she asked.

I tapped my backpack. "Yup. All here, cooked, chilled and ready to serve!"

It was just one stop on the train to the beach (which was actually easier than getting the bus!).

I showed the conductor my photocard, and April May did the same.

Bilal went to show his too, but the conductor just walked into the next carriage.

I burst out laughing.

"It's not funny!" said Bilal. "I'm not **THAT** small!"

April May asked what was going on, so I explained that sometimes the bus drivers and train guards thought that Bilal was a "five and under" and didn't have to pay.

"He doesn't look five!" she said. "I think it might be because you're so tall, Ben."

"Exactly," said Bilal, grinning. "You're a **GIANT**, Ben."

As soon as we got to the beach, it started to rain.

We ran under the toilet shelter.

"Should we just set up here?" Bilal asked.

"Too close to the toilets. That's gross," said April May.

"Well, we don't really have another option while it's raining," I said.

So we dragged some deckchairs over to set up our cold, cooked pizza stall outside the beach toilets.

That's when Kallan and his friends appeared.

"You losers trying to sell pizza next to the toilet block? That's pretty gross," he said. "You want to come with us, April May? Or stay with these losers?"

April May gave Kallan a look.

"Bye, Kallan," she said loudly.

"Fine," he said. "See ya. You lot deserve each other."

Then he **SWIPED** a slice of pizza and ran off laughing.

We stayed there for almost an hour.

But we didn't get one sale.

We were about to pack up and head home when we heard a crowd of people approaching.

"Oh no," said Bilal. "It's the **BINGO LADIES**."

I had no idea what he was talking about until an old woman started shouting, "Bilal! Bilal!"

Suddenly we were surrounded by old women. And they **ALL** seemed to know Bilal!

"How's your mum?" one of them asked.

"Is your brother still at Tesco?"

"Tell your gran we were asking for her!"

"Is she enjoying her cruise?"

Bilal nodded and smiled, but he wasn't really getting a chance to answer.

That's when I remembered that Bilal's gran was obsessed with bingo (and she always seemed to win!).

"Can I have a wee rub for luck, son?" said an old lady, reaching for Bilal's head.

Still smiling, Bilal moved out of the way and put his hood up. "No, but you can have a wee next door."

"Good point, we need to use the ladies'," said one of the bingo crowd. "But we'll be right back!"

"We need to leave **NOW**!" hissed Bilal.

"No way," said April May. "There's loads of them!"

"You don't understand," said Bilal. "They want to **TOUCH** my head."

He explained that his gran was convinced that he was her **GOOD-LUCK CHARM** ever since she rubbed his head before the first **BIG WIN**.

"She literally gets the bus to our house every Saturday morning just so she can rub my head before she goes to bingo!"

That's when the ladies filed out of the toilets and began to swarm around us again.

"So what's all this?" one of them said.

"Pizza!" I said confidently. "Only **£2** a slice!"

I opened the Tupperware box and held up a slice of cold, cooked pizza.

"Can you heat it up?" one woman asked.

"And ruin this delicious flavour?" I said. "Oh no."

Another of the ladies laughed, so I laughed too.

Because the Tank says:

Build up a great rapport with your customers and soon you'll have fans and a social media account where they send you free stuff. But, most importantly, if your first customers like you, they will come back. Got it?

Well, these ladies all **DEFINITELY** liked Bilal.

We made a couple of sales, but the old ladies were more interested in trying to convince Bilal to let them rub his head for good luck.

That's when I had an idea.

"Do you think we could charge them to rub Bilal's head?" I said.

"No," said April May.

"Thank you!" said Bilal, giving me a look.

"But what about some sort of **MEAL DEAL**?" said April May. "Two slices and a head rub for a fiver?"

I stared at Bilal hopefully.

It was his decision.

It was **HIS HEAD**, after all.

Bilal did a loud sigh and pulled his hood down.

"Fine," he said. "But they only get **TWO SECONDS** each, OK?"

"Deal!" I said excitedly.

We sat Bilal on one of the deckchairs. Then I announced the **MEAL DEAL** and a queue started to form.

It worked.

EVERYONE wanted the meal deal!

April May dished out the pizza while I took the cash and Bilal let the bingo ladies rub his head for luck.

"Um, help!" called Bilal.

April May quickly pulled a lady's hand off Bilal's head.

"Time's up," she said. "You'll have to join the queue and buy another two slices if you want more head time."

"That's Betty," said the woman I was serving. "She's desperate for a win this afternoon. She's on a bad-luck streak. Hasn't had a win for over a year now!"

I saw Betty hurry to join the back of the queue.

These women really believed that Bilal's little head had **MAGIC BINGO POWERS**!

I gave Bilal a thumbs up to make sure he was OK.

He gave me an annoyed look for a second, but then he did a thumbs up back so I knew he was OK.

Good old Bilal.

I was surprised he'd been up for it, to be honest.

He was obviously as committed as I was to making this business a success.

But then suddenly Bilal screamed.

The lady I'd just been serving had got her huge ring **STUCK** in his hair!

"Ouch! Stop pulling!" screamed Bilal.

I ran over to help.

April looked at me, panicked.

"I can't get it untangled," she whispered. "I think we're going to need **SCISSORS**."

"What?" shrieked Bilal. "No way!"

I looked at the lady who was now attached to my best friend's head.

"Can you slip your finger out of the ring?" I asked.

The lady laughed. "Son, this ring hasn't come off for years," she said. "Just you wait until you get to my age – your fingers will double in size too!"

That sounded scary (and gross) but I didn't really have time to focus on that.

"She's doing it on purpose!" one of the ladies yelled. "So she gets **EXTRA** time!"

"Well, if she's getting extra time, I want some too!" shouted another.

The crowd got a bit rowdy.

"Who's got nail scissors?" someone yelled.

Loads of them started rummaging around in their handbags.

It worried me that so many of them were carrying weapons. I'd probably never feel safe on the bus again.

I crouched down and looked at Bilal. He was sweating. "Don't cut my hair," he whispered.

April May crouched down next to me.

"It's 12.58 p.m.," she said. "The bingo starts in two minutes. And these ladies are serious about winning. I doubt they're going to wait - even if one of them is attached to you. You're going to get dragged in."

Bilal looked terrified.

"OK. Do the cut," he said.

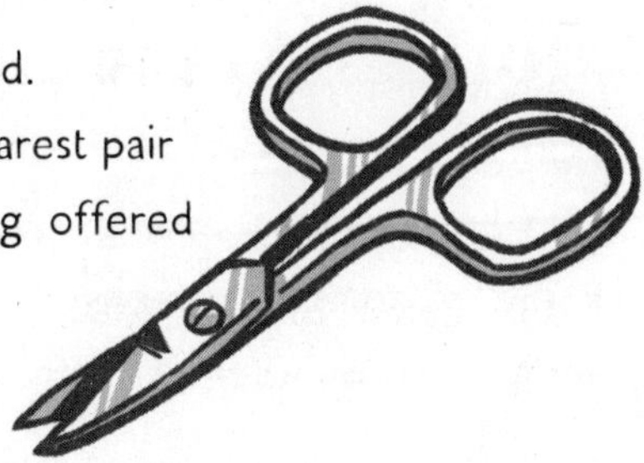

I nodded and took the nearest pair of scissors that were being offered to me.

I looked at April May.

She'd gone a bit pale.

"Don't cut my finger!" said the lady.

I gulped and nodded at her. I didn't want our business to get sued. That could get expensive.

I took a deep breath and tried to get the scissors into position.

"Give them here," said the lady.

She grabbed the scissors out of my hand and -

"There!" she said, removing her hand from Bilal's head.

Me and April May both gasped.

She had a long, thick clump of Bilal's hair sticking out from her ring. And Bilal had a huge chunk of hair missing.

Bilal sat up straight and rubbed the back of his head.

His mouth fell open.

"I can feel my **SCALP**!" he cried.

At that moment, the bingo-hall bell rang and all the ladies turned to go.

"I'm so sorry about that, my darling," said the lady.

She pulled out a **£20** note and handed it to Bilal.

"A hairdresser will be able to fix that, no problem."

"I'm suddenly feeling very **LUCKY**!" she said. "I just know I'm going to win big!"

And then she left.

On the way home, people kept pointing at Bilal's head.

Because he'd decided to cover his hair with a bucket he'd found.

"I'm not using that **£20** for a haircut," said Bilal. "I'll get Yusef to fix it when I get home. And I'm keeping that money!" he added grumpily.

I didn't protest. Bilal deserved it.

I tipped out the money we'd made from selling pizza on to the train table and started to count.

"We made **£100**!" I said.

I couldn't believe it!

"And it's all thanks to you, mate," I said, looking at Bilal.

Bilal gave me a reluctant smile.

"Fine. Make it a hundred and twenty," he said, throwing his twenty on to the pile.

I looked at all the coins and notes on the table.

We'd made **£120**.

In just **TEN MINUTES**.

April May said that there was bingo on a Tuesday night too and that if we hit both bingo sessions every week we could make over **£400** by the end of the month!

"We need more," I said without realizing that I'd just said it.

"We do!" said Bilal. "The Tank always says, there's no ceiling on success."

"Look," said April May. "Am I a proper part of this business now?"

I could see by the look on her face that she really wanted to be part of our business.

And I really wanted her to be part of it too.

I looked at Bilal and he did a tiny nod.

"April May," I said. "You are officially a **PARTNER** in Cheapo Slice O' Pizza. Welcome!"

April May smiled the biggest smile I'd ever seen.

Bilal said, "You'll have to give the business **£10** if you want to be a partner, actually, because that's what we did."

April May nodded and reached into her bag and pulled out a crisp **£10** note.

"Done," she said. "Am I in?"

Bilal and I both nodded.

And so the Future Billionaires' Club got its third member.

"Good," she said. "Because I have an idea that is going to make us a lot of money. Are you busy tomorrow?"

I looked at Bilal and he looked at me and then we both looked at April May and shook our heads.

"Well, you are now," she said.

Then April May grabbed my hand and started writing on my **ARM**.

"Meet me at this address at ten a.m. sharp."

SUNDAY

EIGHT DAYS UNTIL EVICTION

The next morning, Bilal turned up at my front door with a **REVERSE MOHICAN**.

At first I thought it was payback from Yusef for Bilal blaming him for the kitchen mess, but Bilal said that it was what he'd asked for.

"There was no other option," he said. "That bingo lady cut my hair right up to the **SCALP**!"

"What about just getting a skinhead?" I said.

"Mum would go mad if I got a buzz cut," he replied.

"So she's not seen it yet?" I asked.

Bilal shook his head.

I was pretty sure she'd rather he had a buzz cut!

Dad dropped us off at the address April May had given us. A **WAREHOUSE**.

"You sure this is the right place?" he asked. "I thought

you were going to your friend April May's house?"

"Um. So did we," I said.

Suddenly the warehouse doors opened and someone dressed in overalls waved us over.

It was April May.

"There she is!" I said.

Dad rolled down the window and looked out.

"Why are you meeting her here again?" he asked.

I looked at Bilal.

We had no idea.

"Aren't you going to be late for your shift?" said Bilal.

Dad checked the clock on the dashboard, then rushed us out of the car.

"Just phone Mum when you're done and she'll come and get you," he said.

He sped off.

April May had disappeared back inside the warehouse.

"Should we go in?" asked Bilal.

I shrugged. I had no idea what was going on.

April May appeared again a moment later, carrying a huge table.

Bilal raced forward to help her.

"Thanks, Bilal," she said. "Nice hair!"

"Thanks," he said. "I actually quite like it!"

I felt like an idiot for not running over to help too.

I watched as they put the table down next to a van and then April May said, "Follow me."

So we followed her into the warehouse and up a flight of stairs into a little windowed room that looked like a kitchen.

We both stared at April May.

"Where are we?" asked Bilal. "And why are you wearing overalls?"

"This is an auction house," she said. "I work here. My dad owns it."

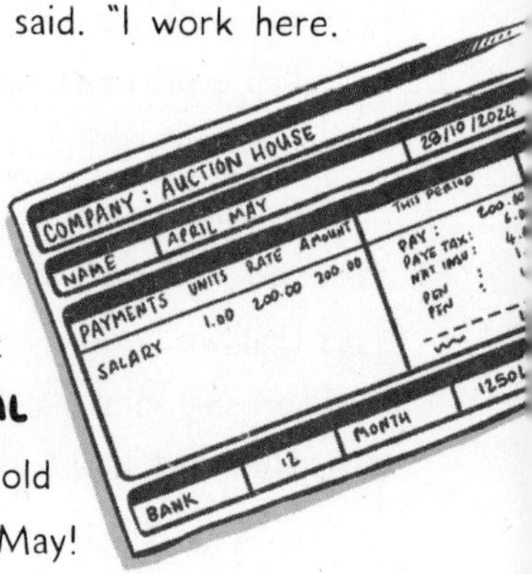

I couldn't believe she had a job!

I mean, she definitely looked a lot older than the rest of us. And she was probably the strongest person I knew. But to have an **ACTUAL JOB** that paid money at ten years old was pretty amazing, even for April May!

"What do you do here?" I asked.

"I'm a **PORTER**," she said. "I help move the furniture on and off the van."

I nodded and tried to look cool, then she asked us if we knew what an auction house was.

We both paused and didn't say anything. Which meant it was pretty obvious that we didn't know.

"People give us their stuff and we sell it for them," April May explained. "People have to bid on stuff. The highest bid wins."

"Oh!" said Bilal. "My mum watches something like that on TV with fancy antiques!"

April May nodded. "Yeah, some of it's good stuff," she said. "But a lot of it's junk. I think people just like the thrill of fighting over things

to see who'll win." She pulled up the blinds and said, "You see that van? That's the coffee man – but he doesn't sell food. I've been saying to Dad for ages that we need a food van for the punters!"

Then she said that in exactly thirty minutes' time **ONE HUNDRED HUNGRY PEOPLE** were going to come flooding out of the warehouse doors.

She pointed to a microwave, then looked at us and said, "You're going to use that to cook one hundred slices of pizza and make **A LOT** of money."

We stared at her.

"Any questions?" she asked.

"Just one," I said. "How are we going to get one hundred slices of pizza?"

April May smiled, then reached behind the counter and pulled out two huge bags.

"Here," she said. "I went shopping this morning. And you guys owe me **£17**," she added. "I kept the receipt."

April May pulled a slip of paper out of her overall pocket and handed it to Bilal, who nodded and wrote something in the notepad that he always carried with him and slipped the receipt inside.

Then April May handed us the two huge bags and ran off, down the stairs and out of sight.

"She runs everywhere. Did you notice that?" said Bilal.

I smiled and nodded.

I **HAD** noticed that.

By the time the warehouse doors opened, we were ready.

Me and Bilal watched as the people came pouring out.

There were a lot of them!

They all rushed to be first in line at the coffee van.

We stood in our matching T-shirts, waiting for one of them to come over.

About the matching T-shirts. The Tank says that you should take every possible opportunity to promote your business. We hadn't had time to get real business T-shirts made up yet, but we both had the same **DINOSAUR**-eating-a-slice-of-pizza T-shirts that Bilal's mum had bought us a couple of summers ago when we went camping together. They were a bit tight but Bilal said that was better because it made us look older and Italian and sophisticated.

I wasn't totally convinced that my belly

button being visible was exactly sophisticated, but we wrote **CHEAPO SLICE O' PIZZA** on them with a Sharpie underneath the dinosaurs and wore them anyway.

The crowd were all pushing in the queue at the coffee van.

But then one of them broke away and started walking towards us.

Our first auction-house customer!

Me and Bilal stood up straight.

The man looked at my belly button and then at the pizza and said, "What's all this?"

"Pizza!" I said cheerfully.

The man gave me a look.

"I mean, we're **CHEAPO SLICE O' PIZZA** - **£2** a slice!"

I could feel Bilal staring at me.

I'd just doubled the agreed price.

But the way I figured it, these were actual grown-ups who obviously had **CASH** to spend if they came here every weekend and bought antique stuff.

The guy looked at the pizza for a second and then he said, "I'll give you **£1.50** for it."

"Make it **£3** and I'll give you two slices," said a voice from behind us.

It was April May.

"This your idea?" the grumpy man said.

April May crossed her arms and said, "Yeah, it is. So you want two slices or should I give them to Frank waiting behind you?"

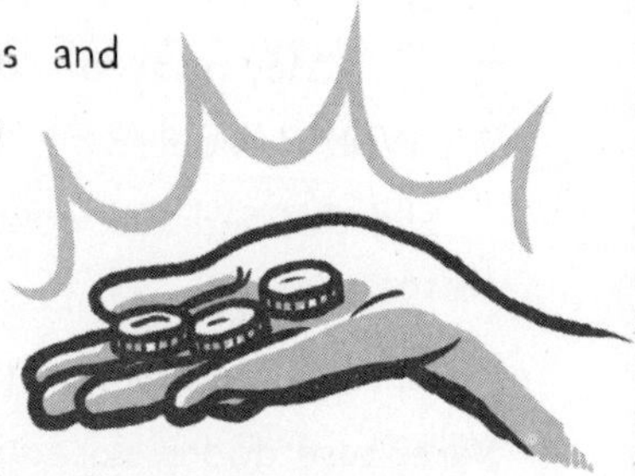

The man handed me **£3** and Bilal gave him two slices of pizza.

It went on like that for ten minutes solid without stopping.

April May made deals over and over again while we took the money and gave out the pizza. Two guys almost started **FIGHTING** over the last two slices until one of them handed us a **FIVER** for them and ran inside.

"I'd better get back in," said April May, wiping pizza grease on her overalls. "You coming again next week?"

I looked at the tub full of cash, then back at April May.

She was smiling. And I'm pretty sure it was because we were both standing with mouths hanging wide open.

"**YES**," I said.

April May nodded and ran off.

"Wait!" I shouted.

She stopped and looked back.

"See you at school tomorrow!"

April May gave us a thumbs up and then pulled the big warehouse doors closed behind her.

MONDAY

SEVEN DAYS UNTIL EVICTION

On the way home from school, we spotted **DAD** sitting in the park.

"Why isn't your dad at work?" Bilal asked.

I didn't know.

I told Bilal to go on without me and that I'd seen him later for our scheduled business meeting. Then I headed into the park, hoping I wouldn't bump into Gael.

Dad looked a bit flustered when he saw me.

"Listen," he said right away. "Don't tell your mum you saw me here, OK?"

He was acting **WEIRD**.

I frowned. I never lie to Mum. (Well, I suppose I do, but I try not to.)

But I wasn't frowning because I didn't like

lying to her. It's because I'm way more scared of upsetting **MUM** than Dad.

"Why aren't you at the factory, Dad?" I asked.

Dad took a deep breath and rubbed his face with both hands, then let out a deep sigh.

"That's the thing," he said. "I don't work there any more. I haven't worked there for months."

I couldn't believe what Dad was saying to me.

It didn't make any sense!

"What do you mean?" I said. "You go to work every day and come home at night!"

I pointed at Dad's clothes. "You're wearing your work clothes right now!"

He nodded and let out another sigh.

That's when he told me that the factory were struggling and that they'd had to let go of a lot of people and that he had been one of those people. He'd been pretending to go to work every day and come home every night at the usual times so that Mum didn't find out.

"I've got my job at the weekends at Starbucks, but I need something else too," he said. "I've been trying, but there just don't seem to be many places hiring a fifty-year-old ex-factory worker."

I wasn't sure what to say.

This was **A LOT**.

"I thought maybe I could start my own business," said Dad. "That was my dream when I was your age, you know. The mongoose farm meant I'd be my own boss. So I took a risk and bought it. And, well, you know the rest."

I watched as Dad looked at the ground.

He was trying hard not to cry.

This was bad.

REALLY BAD.

"I didn't mean to lose all our money," he told me. "I really did believe in that business. I said to myself, 'Well, no one's hiring you and you need a job, so just go for it!' I obviously had no idea it was a scam. I thought it was a way to change things for the better. Maybe even make us all **RICH**!"

I was shocked.

DAD was just like **ME**!

Or I was just like **HIM**.

I'd taken loads of risks for our pizza business because I believed in it.

Dad had believed in the mongoose farm.

He'd been trying to make us rich.

Give us a better life.

Just like I was trying to.

He probably wanted a bigger house with more space and soundproofing like I did!

"Dad," I said. "Can I ask you something?"

Dad nodded.

"Do you think Baby Angel snores loud?" I asked.

Dad laughed.

"YES!" he said.

I was happy to have made him laugh.

"So I'm not the only one, then!" I said.

Dad smiled and grabbed my hand.

"I know I've dumped a lot on you today and that's not fair, I'm sorry. You caught me at a bad moment."

I felt weird.

I mean, I'd been annoyed at Dad for ages about the mongoose-farm thing. But now I didn't feel annoyed at Dad at all.

INSTEAD I felt bad for him. And a bit worried.

Because Dad didn't have a job. He wasn't going to be able to pay the rent like he'd promised. I didn't know how long it would take him to find another one, but I did know one thing for sure.

If I didn't make a lot more money by the end of the week, we were definitely going to get **EVICTED**.

It was up to me.

I knew what I **NEEDED** to do.

AFTER TEA…

I went to see Bilal after tea. There was no time to waste.

"How much money do we have right now?" I asked.

Bilal pulled his little notebook out of his pocket and said, "**£502.**"

That was a lot.

But I needed **DOUBLE** that by the end of the week.

I looked at Bilal.

"I think we need to work harder," I said. "The Tank says to **STRIKE WHILE THE IRON IS BURNING HOT**. We're on to something here. So let's **CRANK IT UP**, yeah?"

I could hear myself. I sounded like the Tank!

Bilal jumped up and shouted, "**YEAH, MAN**!" and high-fived me.

TUESDAY

SIX DAYS UNTIL EVICTION

At lunchtime today, we told April May about **STRIKING WHILE THE IRON IS BURNING HOT**.

And that's when she told us she had a plan to help us make **£1,000** in six days.

I gasped.

This was amazing!

April May said that her plan was for us to sell our pizza to the secondary-school kids on the other side of the fence because they had more money, ate more, and some of the older ones even had jobs!

But that meant that we were going to have to **BREAK THE SCHOOL RULES** by going over the fence.

"We'll get expelled if we

get caught over there, you know that?" said Bilal.

I nodded and so did April May.

Bilal took a deep breath.

"OK then, let's do this!" he said.

Bilal helped me pull the pizza table out from behind the big bush and April May carried the pizza.

We set up next to the bike shed, in case we needed to hide from the teachers, and we waited for the school bell to ring.

I wasn't sure what to expect.

I mean, these were older kids.

They might not want our pizza.

They might laugh at us.

They might beat us up and **STEAL** our pizza!

I was glad April May was with us. She wouldn't let the older kids beat us up.

Suddenly a few kids ran over and April May nudged me.

"Um, we're Cheapo Slice O' Pizza," I said. "You want a slice?"

The boys stared at the pizza. They looked hungry!

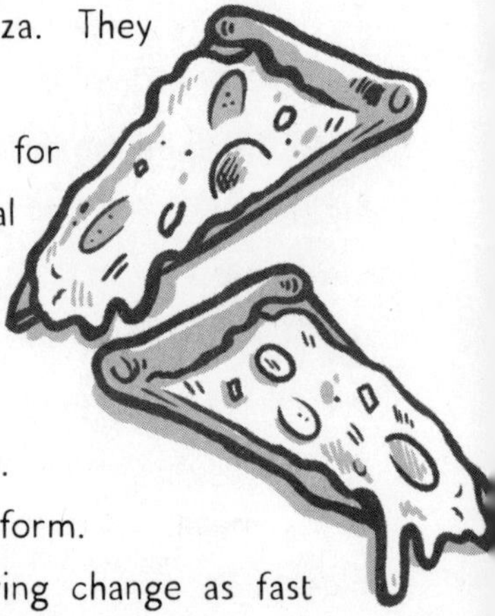

"**£2** a slice or two slices for **£3.50**," said April May. "Total **BARGAIN**. Grab them before they're gone."

It **WORKED**.

The boys bought two slices each.

Then a huge **CROWD** started to form.

Bilal was taking money and giving change as fast as he could and I was serving the pizza faster than I ever had before.

Some kids weren't even taking it away to eat it. They were just eating it really fast right there in front of us!

And others were even coming back for **SECONDS**.

Within five minutes, we were sold out and packing up.

"Hey, will you be back tomorrow?" someone shouted.

"Yes!" April May called out.

FRIDAY

THREE DAYS UNTIL EVICTION

We sold pizza to **BOTH** the high-school and primary-school kids all week.

By the end of Thursday we were up to **£760**.

Bilal said we would probably be up to **£900** once we sold our pizza at the auction house again on Saturday.

But that still meant I would be **£100** short.

Yesterday, after school, I went to Bilal's to see if we could come up with a plan to make the rest before the eviction deadline.

When Bilal answered the door, he was covered in **PAINT**.

"What's going on?" I asked.

Bilal pulled me into the living room.

"I've been painting!" he said.

I expected to see the walls a different colour or something, but instead there were two huge canvases like the ones in art class at school.

"Is that one meant to be **TERRANCE**?" I said.

Bilal shrugged.

"Maybe," he said. "I mean, it is if you want it to be and it isn't if you don't."

I looked at the other one. It was a bit like Bilal if he were inside a washing machine.

I asked Bilal if he was feeling OK.

He said that he was.

I asked him why he had done this.

And that's when he said, "I did it for **YOU**!"

I panicked. I had no idea where I was going to put a **GIANT WEIRD** painting. And I was pretty sure Mum wouldn't be happy about it.

But then again...

Terry was now sleeping in the bed with her and I'm pretty sure I saw her brushing his teeth in the bathroom this morning.

So maybe she would be happy to have a massive abstract

painting of him at home (as she was clearly becoming obsessed with him).

"Do you like them?" asked Bilal.

I looked down at Bilal's paint-covered face.

"They're ... well ... **WOW!**" I said.

I had no idea what else to say.

I mean, Bilal was my best friend and he was obviously just trying to be nice by painting these monstrosities for me.

All I could do was smile and say thank you and think of a way to accidentally on purpose set them on fire.

Obviously.

"Thanks for making these for me, Bilal," I said. "I'm not sure where I'll put them but—"

Bilal stared at me.

"They're not for you to keep!" he said. "They're for the business!"

"I'm hoping April May will let me try to sell them at the auction house," Bilal explained.

"She said people bid on all sorts of stuff and that got me thinking. You know those paintings that don't look like anything? We learnt about them in art."

I nodded.

"Well!" said Bilal, pointing his paintbrush at the canvases. "I thought I could **DO** that. So I did!"

I looked at the paintings.

"They're awful, aren't they?" said Bilal.

I looked at Bilal.

He was smiling but I wasn't sure whether he really thought they were awful or whether he was just saying that because he was worried that I might think they were.

I mean, they were awful. But, then again, I thought some of the ones we were shown in art class were actually worse!

I put my hand on my best friend's shoulder. He must have stayed up all night making these for us to sell.

He was a good friend.

My **BEST** friend.

"No, Bilal," I said. "They're not awful. They're **ABSTRACT**."

Bilal beamed at me.

"Do you really think so?" he said.

I nodded.

Because I really did.

*

We weren't able to sell our pizza at school today.

Word had spread to the **DINNER LADIES** about an **ILLEGAL PIZZA BUSINESS** and they were patrolling the playground!

Bilal and April May and I ate as much of the pizza as we could and then put the rest in the bin.

Things were also starting to get tricky with cooking the pizza in the staffroom. We couldn't keep taking turns asking to go to the toilet before the lunch bell. Mrs Knot was obviously getting suspicious.

"We can't keep this up," said Bilal. "We need a new plan."

That's when April May said that she had a **NEW** idea.

"Why don't we serve it cold, like we did at the beach?" she said. "We could all cook as much as we can at home the night before, and we could use ice packs to keep it cold afterwards. Then, when we come into school, the pizza would be cooked, cut and ready to serve. We could get rid of it in **MINUTES** and not get caught!"

I wasn't sure that people would want to buy cold pizza. The only reason the bingo ladies had bought it was because they really wanted to rub Bilal's head.

But then April May said that she thought cold pizza was actually more delicious than hot pizza, and Bilal agreed!

Bilal took out his notepad and starting doing **THE NUMBERS**.

Then he gasped and said, "According to my calculations and the available volume space in three school backpacks, we could carry at least a hundred slices of cooked pizza each!"

That would be a **GAME CHANGER**. We could make more money selling cold pizza.

But then I realized it didn't matter. Because today was Friday. I only had the weekend to make enough money to avoid losing my home.

Which meant I had two days to make the rest of the money.

SATURDAY

TWO DAYS UNTIL EVICTION

So now it was all down to how much pizza we could sell on Saturday at the auction.

"We need another **£240**," I told Bilal. Then I remembered that Bilal didn't know about the rent money, so I said, "I mean, I think that's what we should aim for anyway. The Tank says it's good to be specific in your aims."

"We'll manage it," Bilal said. "After all, we've got my paintings too."

I wasn't sure they would sell for more than the pizza, but I gave him an encouraging smile.

Bilal said that April May was going to put his paintings into the auction.

I could hardly breathe when the auction doors opened at the break.

And it wasn't just because I'd spotted April May.

It was because it felt like my entire life was riding

on whether or not these grumpy-looking men wanted our pizza.

And that's when we hit a **PROBLEM**.

People weren't coming over.

They were staying at the coffee van.

"What's going on?" said Bilal.

I shrugged. I didn't know.

I saw April May charge over to the coffee van and start shouting at the guy!

I had no idea what was going on until I saw one of the grumpy men holding a cup of coffee and a slice of PIZZA.

The coffee guy had STOLEN our business!

We rushed over – and I saw Kallan inside the van! He was wearing an apron and cooking pizzas in the microwave!

"Oh, hello," said Kallan.

"What are you doing here?" I said.

"This is my Uncle Dougal's van,"

he said. "He mentioned there were some **LOSERS** here last week trying to sell awful pizza ... so I thought I'd be helpful and come and give the people something better!"

Kallan grinned and held up a **PEPPERONI** pizza.

April May was going mad, telling him to stop right now or else!

But he didn't stop.

He just said, "It's a free country. My uncle can serve pizza with his coffee if he wants."

Bilal pulled at my sleeve and pointed to the side of the van.

He'd stolen our idea! Our business! Our **NAME**!

"Let's slash our prices. Quick!" said Bilal.

So we did that.

I mean, we had to. All the hot pizza was going to go to waste and if I didn't make **£240** today I would be homeless!

We made a few sales, but by the end of the break we'd only made **£30**.

It was a **DISASTER**.

I sat down on the ground and watched the coffee van drive away with all the money that should have been ours.

Bilal was counting the money and doing calculations in his notepad.

Suddenly Bilal said, "We need more. The Tank says we should squeeze every opportunity dry."

And then he reached into his backpack and pulled out a pair of trainers and handed them to April May. She nodded and ran back inside.

"Limited edition. Impossible to get," Bilal said. "They're Yusef's."

"Does he know you're selling them?" I asked.

"No," said Bilal. "He's got loads. He doesn't need them."

I had no idea why Bilal seemed to have a death wish, but before I could quiz him about it there was a really loud whistle. We jumped and saw April May over

by the warehouse door, frantically waving.

We ran over.

"Quick!" she said, grabbing Bilal. "What's the title of the painting that looks like your face stuck inside a washing machine?"

A laugh burst out of me. I couldn't help it! That's **EXACTLY** how I would have described the painting!

"Um ... I don't know!" said Bilal. "Wait, um, I'll call it ... **DEEP CLEAN**."

April May nodded and ran back inside, but then her head poked out again.

"Do **YOU** have a name?"

Bilal looked confused.

"What's your **ARTIST** name? What do you want to be called? People are asking!"

"Um ... Let me think ... **BLT!**" said Bilal.

April May nodded and disappeared again.

"BLT," I echoed.

"I panicked," said Bilal. "But it's sort of arty, isn't it?"

I looked at Bilal. "You know a BLT is a bacon, lettuce and tomato sandwich, right?"

Bilal looked surprised.

"Oh," he said. "No, I didn't know that." And then he started laughing. "I just thought it sounded good!"

April May appeared yet again. This time she had a **PANICKED** look on her face.

"You'd better come inside," she said.

Something was obviously wrong. I'd never seen April May look like that before. She was usually unflappable!

We hurried inside and that's when we saw one of Bilal's paintings on a big **SCREEN**.

There were numbers across the screen. In front of it was a large man standing on a stage. He was shouting into the room, and loads of people were raising their hands.

Then the numbers on the screen started getting higher and higher.

"We just started doing online bids too," said April May. "The people in the room are bidding against people all over the UK. And maybe even other parts of the world."

We stared at the screen, showing a picture of Bilal's weird **DEEP CLEAN** painting.

"I have **£100**. Do I see one hundred and ten?" said the large man at the front.

I gasped.

April May nodded. "And we're not finished yet," she said. "It's still going!"

"I have **£110** online from a bidder in Japan. Do I see one hundred and twenty, please?"

I stared at Bilal. He looked like he was going to faint.

"I have **£120**, thank you. How about one hundred and forty?"

One of the grumpy old men put his hand up.

I couldn't believe this was happening!

"It's against you online," said the auctioneer. "I have a bid of **£200** here from Italy."

The grumpy man put his hand up again.

"Thank you, sir," said the auctioneer. "I now have **£220** in the room."

A lady at the back put up her hand. She looked a bit familiar.

"I have **£240**. Do I see two hundred and fifty anywhere?"

No one else put their hand up.

"I have **£240**. Are there any more bids? If not, then I'm going to sell to the bidder at the back of the room for **£240**..."

I jumped as the auctioneer slammed his hammer down.

"**SOLD!**" he cried.

I turned to Bilal and April May.

"I can't believe it!" I managed to say.

"I'm an artist!" said Bilal.

I started laughing.

I couldn't believe it. We'd **DONE IT**. We'd made over **£1,000**!

"And your trainers went for **£600** to the arty guy sitting at the front!" April May told Bilal.

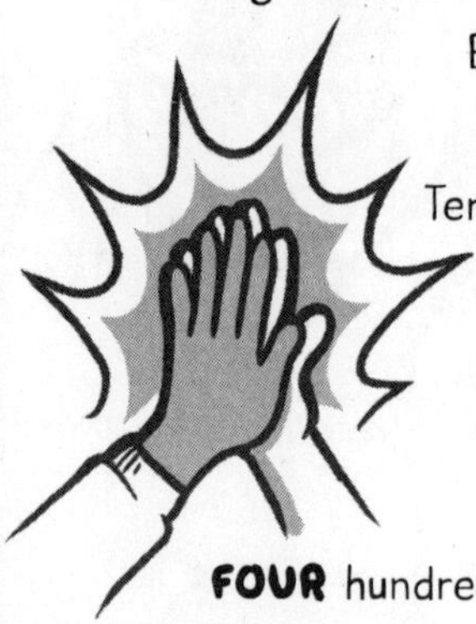

Bilal gave April May a high five.

Next, his bizarre painting of sort-of-Terrance flashed on to the screen.

I held my breath and watched.

One hundred.

Two hundred.

Three hundred.

FOUR hundred.

Five.

Six.

Bilal sunk to the floor and I joined him.

This was too much!

Seven.

Eight.

NINE HUNDRED.

"**SOLD** to the gentleman in the front row for **£1,000**!" the auctioneer cried.

Oh.

My.

Gosh.

"What just happened?!" I said. "Is that real?"

"It's real," April May said, smiling. Then she turned to Bilal. "You're going to be rich, BLT!"

Bilal stared at us both. "Me? You mean **WE'RE** going to be rich. Those are **BUSINESS** paintings."

We all stumbled outside for some fresh air.

"**WE DID IT!**" Bilal screamed, raising his hands and dropping to his knees.

"I've never seen anything like that," said April May. "Do you think you could paint more?"

"Yes, I can!" yelled Bilal, laughing.

I burst out laughing too.

Bilal was going wild.

I lay down on the ground.

We'd done it. We had really **DONE** it.

"Thank you, Tank!" I shouted up at the sky. "And thank you, BLT!" I shouted even louder.

Bilal laughed and lay down beside me.

April May looked at us with a huge smile on her face.

"What now?" said Bilal. "Do we stop doing the pizza and

just do the paintings?"

"No way," said April May, lying down beside us as well. "We're Cheapo Slice O' Pizza **FOR EVER**! This is my dad's auction house. I'm going to make sure that coffee guy never sells another cup of coffee here ever again after trying to steal our business like that!"

"Hey!" I said. "Maybe we could do the coffee and the pizza!"

"I love it, I love it, **I LUUUUUUUUUVE IIIIIIIIT!**" screamed Bilal.

He really was going wild!

"What's wrong with you?" I said, laughing.

"We just became thousand-aires!" he said, breathless now. "That's what!"

I thought about what Bilal had said.

We **HAD** just become **THOUSAND-AIRES**.

That wasn't quite a **BILLIONAIRE**, but we were on our way!

"We can do pizza and paintings!" said Bilal.

"You know, I have other ideas for our business too," said April May.

I laughed out loud. This was **AMAZING**.

"I never thought that when Dad told us he'd bought a fake mongoose farm and lost ten thousand pounds it would lead to this!"

April May was staring at me, so I explained the whole **MONGOOSE** fiasco to her.

She jumped up. Her eyes were wide.

"Does your dad own the land?" she asked.

"Yes," I said. "But there's absolutely nothing on it – it's just a small bit of empty land. And there's definitely no mongoose!"

"Not even one mongoose!" Bilal added.

I had no idea why April May was interested in the non-mongoose farm.

"But it's land, right?" said April May. "And your dad has the deed?"

I nodded.

April May made me tell her everything I knew about the fake mongoose farm, like where it was and how big it was and how much my dad had paid for it.

"Has he tried to sell it?" she asked.

I remembered Dad telling Mum and the police that he'd tried to sell it, but no one was interested because it was so small and in the middle of nowhere. He said it was unsellable.

April May grinned.

"Trust me," she said. "Nothing is unsellable!"

And then she ran off.

We got up and ran after her into the auction house.

Inside, April May handed me a phone and said, "Get your dad on the phone, then give the phone to my dad. We need the deed now. We're going to sell that land and get your dad's money back!"

I called Dad and then April May marched us over to her dad (who was wearing a very jazzy tie) and explained about the land and then handed him the phone.

We watched as April May climbed up to the little stage and whispered something into the auctioneer's ear.

The auctioneer shook his head.

But April kept whispering and she pointed at her dad, who was busy talking to my dad on the phone. Then April May's dad ended the call and gave April May a thumbs up.

"Ladies and gentlemen!" April May **BOOMED** down the microphone. "It appears that we have one final exciting lot for your bidding pleasure today."

The crowd all shifted in their seats and mumbled to each other. They were obviously excited.

"Lot 556 today is a piece of **LAND**," April May announced.

The crowd gasped.

"It's a small piece of desirable land in the beautiful Welsh countryside."

The online bidding went **WILD**.

A number flashed across the screen.

April May froze.

Then she kicked into gear.

"Thank you. I'll start the bidding at **£3,000**. Can I have **FOUR THOUSAND** next, please?"

The screen flashed:

Bilal put his arms round me and gripped me tight.

I wasn't sure if he was hugging me or holding himself up so he didn't faint.

April May caught my eye from the stage. She was thinking the same as me. This was **ACTUALLY** happening.

"I have **£5,000** from one of our many bidders in America. Lots of interest there! Do I see eight thousand, please?"

A man in the room put his hand up.

"Thank you!" April May shouted into the microphone. "I have **£8,000** in the room. Do I see—"

She didn't even get to finish her sentence.

The amount

appeared on the screen.

The crowd gasped.

April May's dad leapt on to the stage. "We're having some technical difficulties with our online bidding system. Bidding will resume shortly."

I stood there, stunned, as April May stepped down from the stage and joined me and Bilal.

"What's going on?" said Bilal. "Did we sell it?"

"Not yet," said April May. "Dad's buying us some time to let Ben's dad get here with the deed. We can't sell it without that land deed."

A few minutes later, Dad came

rushing in with his Starbucks apron still on, waving the deed in the air and gasping for a breath.

April May rushed back onstage.

"Welcome back, ladies and gentlemen. We currently have a bid of **£20,000** online. Do I see **TWENTY-FIVE**?"

The screen flashed:

£25,000

"I have **£25,000** from one of our American bidders. Do I see **THIRTY** anywhere?"

There were no more bids.

"OK. Then I'm selling the lovely small plot of land in the wonderful Welsh countryside to our American bidder for **£25,000**. Going once. Going twice—"

"**£50,000!**" someone yelled from the back of the room.

It was **MY DAD**!

Everyone gasped and turned round to see who had bid.

Next to me, Dad gave me a nervous smile.

"I changed my mind," he said. "I don't want to sell the land. I want to turn it into a business! I can do it. I know I can!"

April May's dad nodded at April May and she shouted, "Um ... **SOLD!** That's all, folks! Thank you for coming today. See you next week!"

I looked at Dad.

He was just standing there. Not moving.

I reached out and put my hand on his arm.

"You did the right thing," I said.

Dad snapped out of his trance and looked down at me.

"Do you think so?" he said.

I nodded that I did (even though I wasn't completely sure I believed that!) – but I knew that it was what he needed to hear.

April May ran off and then she reappeared with a cheque and handed it to me.

It was for **£1,840**.

I stared at the cheque and that's when I noticed

that it had Dad's name on it.

It was all the money that we'd made today from the art and the trainers.

And it was in Dad's name.

I looked up at Bilal and April May.

They were both smiling widely.

"That's all the money from the art and the trainers," said Bilal. "We want you and your dad to have it all."

"I even convinced my dad not to take our usual percentage," said April May. "It's all yours."

"Wait," I said slowly.

Just then Yusef came barging in, demanding to know where his trainers were.

"You!" he yelled at Bilal. "Mum said you were here. Where are my trainers?"

"I sold them," said Bilal.

Yusef lunged at Bilal – but April May was quicker.

She leapt forward and twisted Yusef's arm behind his back and kept it there in an arm hold.

"Just listen," she said.

And that's when Bilal told Yusef that he needed the money. He looked at me, then back at Yusef and said, "Otherwise Ben and his family are going to get kicked out of their flat, OK?"

I was shocked.

They knew.

They **BOTH** knew!

That's why Bilal had looked stressed when he was counting the money outside. And why he'd stolen Yusef's trainers and put them up for auction.

"How did you find out?" I asked.

"I overheard your mum telling my mum," said Bilal. "I told April May at the beach that day. We wanted to help."

Just then a man appeared, holding one of Bilal's paintings.

"Are you wearing my trainers, mate?" Yusef yelped.

"I won these," said the man. "I also won this wonderful painting and I believe that you might be the artist," he said, looking at Bilal hopefully.

Bilal nodded, and the arty guy said that he ran an art gallery. He thought that Bilal had great potential and that he'd be keen to see more of his work right away.

"I actually tried to convince that lady over there to let me buy your other piece. I offered her a large sum of money, but she refused to part with it! She believes it to be some form of good-luck charm!"

I looked over at the lady holding the washing-machine painting. It was one of the **BINGO LADIES**!

"There will a new piece next Sunday," said April May. "Isn't that right, BLT?"

Bilal nodded.

The arty man looked delighted!

"Well ... I'll be here!" he said, and turned to leave.

"Dude, do not try to walk off wearing my shoes!!" said Yusef.

So that's when Bilal had a quiet word with the arty man, and we all watched as the arty man nodded eagerly, then took the trainers off and handed them to Bilal.

"There you go," said Bilal. "I traded them for my next work of art."

April May released Yusef. He grabbed his trainers and stormed off in a huff.

"Thank so much, guys," I said. "I'm going to go and give this to my dad."

When I explained and gave Dad the

cheque he started laughing.

And then he started crying.

Then laughing again.

It was weird.

But it was good.

"Dad! Dad!" I said, trying to get his attention between all the tears and laughs. "Let's go and tell Mum we're not getting evicted!"

Dad and I burst through the door.

But before we could say anything, Mum screamed, "**I WON! I WON, PATRICK!**"

I had no idea what Mum had won.

For a second I thought she might have won the lottery because she was screaming the house down!

"**LOOK! LOOK!**" she yelled.

Mum shoved a letter into Dad's face.

Dad pulled the letter back and read it. Then he started screaming too!

Mum had sent part of her book off to a competition and she had **WON**! Now a big London agent wanted to read the full book and bring her down to London to speak about helping her get it published!

"I'm getting my own mentor who's going to help me!" she squealed. "And I get to go to London and stay in a fancy hotel and meet all these fancy book people!"

"Right, that's it!" said Dad. "This calls for **CHAMPAGNE**!"

Mum laughed and clapped her hands, and Terrance started barking his head off.

I couldn't believe it.

Mum's book had won!

"Well done, Mum!" I said. "I know I'm not allowed to read it because of all the murder and stuff, but I think it's going to be a bestseller!"

Mum grabbed me and hugged me and held on for ages.

Then she looked at me and said, "You OK?"

"Me?" I said.

"Yes, you," she said, rubbing my hair.

"I'm very OK!" I said, grinning.

I looked up at Dad.

I couldn't wait for him to tell Mum about the **CHEQUE**.

But he didn't.

He just said, "Wait right there!"

Then he ran down to the shops and came back with a

bottle of champagne and one of the really expensive pizzas!

Dad opened the champagne. The cork went flying and hit the ceiling and Mum screamed and laughed and Terrance ran around searching for the cork.

But Dad **STILL** didn't say anything.

I waited until Aunty Gemma arrived and Mum was busy showing her the fancy letter. Then I pulled Dad into the hall and asked him why he hadn't shown Mum the cheque yet!

"This is Mum's night," he said. "She deserves all the attention."

I looked at Mum and Aunty Gemma jumping up and down, spilling the champagne everywhere. Terrance was jumping up and down too, trying to grab the pizza from Aunty Gemma's hand.

"We will tell her, Ben. And I'm going to come clean about losing my job too. Just give her a minute. She's loving this. And, listen, there's something I want to say."

He turned me round so he could look at me.

"I'm so happy that we have the money for the rent and I'm sorry to have put you in a position where you took that on yourself. I panicked. But I won't let that happen again, I promise. No more buying mongoose farms without talking it through first. I'm starting to realize that some things are more important than money."

He was watching Mum and smiling.

"Like people, and love and your dreams!" he said.

I thought about Bilal and how he had stayed up all night making those paintings for me.

And about how April May had tried to sell the plot of land for me.

"Yeah, I know that," I said.

And I meant it.

But...

I was still going to become a ten-year-old **BILLIONAIRE**.

Pamela Butchart is an award winning, best-selling children's author. She lives in Dundee with her son, her fiancé and their very loud cat, Bear. If she wasn't a writer and philosophy teacher, she'd probably open a luxury hotel for stray cats. Her top-selling stories include *The Spy Who Loved School Dinners*, which won the Blue Peter Best Story Award, *My Head Teacher is a Vampire Rat*, which won the Children's Book Award and *A Monster Ate My Packed Lunch*, which won the Lollies – the Laugh Out Loud Awards.

Craig 'wotto' Watkins is an illustrator based in California, where he lives with his wife, two kids and four cats (Goose, Duck, Frog & Toad). Wotto grew up in England where he was inspired by street art, comic books and skateboard graphics. From these early influences he developed a distinctive doodley illustrative style. Wotto's work has rich colour palettes, unique characters with funny sometimes ridiculous narratives. He loves to draw ghosts, skulls, pears and mushrooms.

ACKNOWLEDGEMENTS

Thanks so much to everyone who helped bring Ben and Bilal into the world. My agent Becky, my editor Polly, cover and inside illustrator Wotto, Linas, Wendy, Sarah, and designer Jamie ... THANK YOU. You've all done such an amazing job and I couldn't be more proud of what we've created. Cheapo Slice O' Pizza for EVERYONE!

Thank you to all the young people I've taught over the years who inspired me and made me laugh out loud.

Thanks to Khan's of Broughty Ferry for fuelling my midnight pen.

Thank you to my wonderful fiancé, Chae, for your love and support (and all the LISTENING) while I found my way with the book. And for the many, many midnight trips to the takeaway.

Most of all, thank you to Albie. The funniest guy in the universe. You inspire Mummy every day. I love you.